CHEAP HEAT

Also by Daniel M. Ford

THE JACK DIXON SERIES

Body Broker

THE PALADIN TRILOGY

Ordination
Stillbright
Crusade

CHEAP HEAT

A Jack Dixon Novel
DANIEL M. FORD

sfwp.com

Library of Congress Cataloging-in-Publication Data
Names: Ford, Daniel M., 1978- author.
Title: Cheap heat : a Jack Dixon novel / Daniel M. Ford.
Description: Santa Fe, NM : Santa Fe Writers Project, [2020] | Series: Jack
    Dixon | Summary: "Jack Dixon takes his PI talents on the road when a pro
    wrestler's outlandish Civil War-themed act results in death threats.
    Jack accompanies the self-styled "U.S. Grant" — an old college buddy —
    and his regional wrestling promotion on their fall tour in hopes of
    sniffing out the mystery and escaping his troubled past...and to avoid
    any more harrowing run-ins with the deadly Aesir gang. Struggling with a
    budding romance, the specter of his college-era mistakes, and the
    undercurrents of a fanatic pro wrestling fandom, some of whom may just
    be willing to kill, Jack soon finds himself dragged into the limelight -
    and squarely into the crosshairs of his most dangerous enemies"—
    Provided by publisher.
Identifiers: LCCN 2019022790 (print) | LCCN 2019022791 (ebook) | ISBN
    9781733777711 (trade paperback) | ISBN 9781733777728 (kindle edition)
Subjects: GSAFD: Mystery fiction. | Suspense fiction.
Classification: LCC PS3606.O728 C48 2020 (print) | LCC PS3606.O728
    (ebook) | DDC 813/.6—dc23
LC record available at https://lccn.loc.gov/2019022790
LC ebook record available at https://lccn.loc.gov/2019022791

Published by SFWP
369 Montezuma Ave. #350
Santa Fe, NM 87501
(505) 428-9045
www.sfwp.com

To Gary, for the scotch. And to the rest of the Craigcon crew, I guess.

Chapter 1

Asteady gray rain fell, the kind of cold pelting rain that made everyone who was forced to be out in it miserable, and everyone who had a roof glad to huddle under it, preferably in front of a heater or a fireplace.

It drummed off my helmet and streaked down the visor. It kept up a steady noise that must've driven my boss, on the open end of a phone call via the helmet's Bluetooth, nuts.

I couldn't have been happier.

Despite only having owned It for a couple of months, I found riding so infinitely preferable to driving that I couldn't believe I hadn't bought a motorcycle sooner. I'd thought all the talk about the freedom and comfort and joy of it to be just so much bullshit, but every bit of it turned out to be true for me. The bike—a recent, not vintage, Indian Scout—had proven to be as right for me as living on my boat had been.

So, naturally, my boss found ways to take advantage of it at every turn.

"You got the tracker on yet or what?"

Jason's voice crackled inside my helmet. There was an echoey quality to it that told me he had it on speakerphone. Our principal was probably in the room with him. Maybe another employee.

"I can get it at the next traffic light." I was on Route 40 in Cecil County, Maryland, but probably heading for the Hatem bridge and the Harford County line. "Why don't I just follow this guy all the way to his destination?"

"Because he'll notice the biker in the nerd helmet following him eventually. Especially if you pull into the same parking lot he does. And because this isn't about confronting him."

"Fine, fine." By then the light had changed and the sedan I was tailing from two cars and one lane away had started off again.

I picked up speed, signaled to get into his lane with one hand, and hoped the driver that stood in my way wasn't the kind who aimed at motorcyclists. They were out there, or so I'd been told, but I had yet to experience that kind of malice, only the occasional moment of negligence. Usually when a driver was looking at their phone instead of me.

From what I could see in the front of the Audi I was tailing, the driver was not busy with his phone. He was distracted, certainly, but it seemed more to do with the woman in the passenger seat. At least one of her hands was in his lap, and one of his hands roamed freely inside her coat.

"I don't think he's gonna notice me," I said. "He, uh, seems pretty occupied." There was a discreet cough over the phone connection.

Oh, I thought. *Right. His wife is listening.*

I took it pretty slow to stay behind him. I was pretty sure I could've taken care of this and sped off with a backfire and as much rumble as I could pull out of my bike's engine, but orders were orders.

We were coming up on another red light. He was going slow enough now—his head was rolling back on the headrest—that the other cars behind us had long since shifted into other lanes and passed. The light was barely yellow but he stopped anyway. Probably on the edge of losing fine motor control. His companion's arm was pumping a little more furiously now.

The driver's seat was, in fact, rocking a bit.

As we stopped at the light I inched up closer and closer. Then I bent down as if I had to check my boot laces or something on my bike.

And while I bent down, I slipped a small magnetic case out of my pocket. I leaned forward and slipped it under the bumper of the Audi. It seated home easily.

The light changed. The car took off.

"Is it broadcasting?"

"U-turn at the next opportunity and we'll be sure."

I did as he asked, turning onto a mostly empty road. Early Tuesday afternoons as gray and cold and miserable as this one don't often see a lot of traffic.

"We got him."

"Am I off the clock, then?"

"Seeing as how you can't take photos worth a damn on your phone, and there's no room on that ridiculous vehicle for a camera bag, yes. We'll have someone else stake out the stopping point."

Given the number of motels, hotels, and B&Bs in the direction that Audi had been headed, the couple with cheating on their minds was limited only by their budget and imagination. And since it was a late model Audi with what appeared to be lots of bells and whistles, budget didn't seem like a problem.

"Thank you, Mr. Dixon," said an unfamiliar voice. The wife who was, even now, being humiliated while her husband broke vows they'd made together. She seemed to be holding it together well.

"You're welcome, Mrs. Jackson," I said.

"We're signing off now, Jack," Jason said. Then the line went dead.

Suddenly the rain felt a lot colder and I was glad to be heading home.

Chapter 2

Home wasn't exactly warm, though. There were only so many hatches I could shut and tarps I could put up, and I didn't like running the heater too hot or too long. Not least because if I did, Marty—the manager who handled my arrangement with the marina—would realize I was home and probably come bother me about helping him with something.

Technically, a certain number of hours of manual labor a month were a part of my rent. I entertained myself by avoiding it at all costs.

So it was a bit chilly inside the *Belle of Joppa* this time of year. And in another month or so, shipboard living might become entirely untenable unless I made some investments in equipment or was prepared to run the climate control a lot more than I liked to. Last winter was the first I'd lived aboard her, and I had been lucky enough for it to be a mild one. Still, in layers—a t-shirt, a thick thermal Henley, a fleece vest—the drumming of the rain outside my sealed compartments wasn't entirely unpleasant.

The prospect of Thanksgiving being only a week and two days away didn't *precisely* thrill me, though. I was certainly expected to show up at my family dinner, at my parents' house in Perry Hall. But I was starting to think that things were going too well for me to bother spending any time around my dad. I'd have to think on that some more, but for now,

I decided to think about the Saturday after Thanksgiving. That was the day I truly looked forward to, the balm after dealing with my dad. But before that could get here, I had an important question to ask.

I was, even now, beginning preparations in that vein. The bar was open and a pair of cocktails were taking shape in the galley. I squeezed out some blood orange halves, then pressed ice-spheres—really ice Death Stars, if I were being completely honest—into the oranges so that the peel enveloped half the ice. I placed one in each glass, then I mixed bourbon, smoked tea liqueur, and bitters with ice in the shaker. A few seconds of brisk mixing later, and I was pouring the two drinks through a strainer, over the ice and blood orange.

I clicked on a few electric candles—no open flames on my *Belle*—and then retrieved a wide-brimmed fishing hat, my rain coat, and an umbrella from where I'd stashed them, and headed out into the parking lot.

When a silvery-blue Honda pulled up, I was already standing by with the umbrella open. Gen got out in her own ankle-length rain coat and immediately ducked under it.

"You know, Jack, dinner nights on your boat seemed a lot more romantic in October weather than they do now."

"I bet I can change your mind," I said, as we walked the short distance to my slip. Once we both got inside and had our rain jackets off and the umbrella and hat safely stowed, I took just one moment to look at her.

Even at the end of a workday, with rain flattening her short blonde hair and the fatigue of the office wearing on her, Geneva Lawton was a beautiful woman. She'd let her hair grow a little, although even dry and loose it wouldn't have reached her chin. Her cheeks were smooth, the tan she cultivated with weekly running starting to fade since it was late fall, but her skin still had a glow. Her eyes were large and brown and deep and focused on me for reasons I could not really fathom.

I handed one of the cocktails to her.

"What's this," she said, smelling it, still eyeing me over the rim.

"A Ghost Story," I said. "Blood orange, bourbon, smoked tea liqueur." She took a sip. She smiled. My heart did a little flip.

She turned around to look at the candles I'd laid out, the cheeseboard on the dinner table—which, for once, had been cleared of books—and the ramekins flanking it, with olives, a spicy mustard, and a garlic mayo—and sighed.

"You do make this look better than I'd think it could," Gen admitted.

"Not nearly as good as it looks when you're here," I said. I set my drink down and slid an arm around her back. She slid up against me and we kissed. It was a good kiss, as end-of-work-day kisses went. I would say that it suggested but didn't necessarily promise anything more. I enjoyed it.

She slid away from me and sipped her cocktail again and eyed the cheese I'd set out, then slid her brown eyes back to me.

"BellaVitano raspberry," I said, pointing to a hard cheese with a dark purple rind. "And just a little bit of D'Affinois Double Creme." That was a soft cheese, pale yellow and just oozing out of its rind.

She sampled both, using the cheese knives I'd set out, nodding approvingly, watching me with a smile in her eyes the whole time.

"You know," she said, "it's a little cold to have just cheese and crackers for dinner."

"Which is why I'm making Galician Broth," I said.

"And that is?"

"Some ham, some cannellini beans, potatoes, some garlic, cumin, Spanish paprika, homemade broth…"

"You made broth in *here*?" Gen gestured to my galley, which wasn't much bigger than a half-bath in most suburban houses.

"Every few months Dani lets me use her kitchen to make a few giant stock-pots of the stuff. She keeps it in her deep freeze and I take some now and then."

We ate a little more cheese and then I started getting ingredients out of my tiny fridge, and gathering a pot from the rack above the stove. How the designers got four burners on it I don't know, but they did.

"Speaking of Dani's house," I said casually as I turned a burner on and set the pot on it, followed by a quickly chopped handful of garlic cloves.

"Yes?"

"Well, next Saturday…two days after Thanksgiving. We kind of… do a thing."

I heard her stand up and slide up behind me. She put her arms on the back of my shoulders and leaned her head against the back of my neck.

"You're so bashful when you try to ask me to things. It's cute."

I felt my cheeks go absolutely nuclear. I did not quite know how to handle compliments from Gen, though she wasn't shy about offering them.

"Well," I said, slowing but not stopping the rhythm of my knife through a potato, "it would be great if you could come. It's a little bit of a second Thanksgiving."

"Who'll be there?"

"Me, Dani, Emily, usually people from their church and neighborhood. Maybe one of Dani's veteran friends if they're in town."

"That where you met Dani? The Navy?"

Gen and Dani had met in passing, at the gym, but they hadn't had a long face to face. I wasn't quite sure how to bring the two of them together. It had bested better men than me.

"Nope." I set my knife down and turned around, carefully, so that I had my arms around her again and was facing her. "I've known Dani since we were sophomores in high school."

"How'd you meet?"

"Church function. Then I took her to homecoming," I said.

She chuckled softly and patted me on the cheek. "That must've been an interesting date."

"Eye opening, sure. She made it clear she didn't want to go on another, but we liked a lot of the same things...books, sports, MMA..." I shrugged. "Helped me realize that there wasn't really a whole lot in gender and friendship, you know? A person is a person, you get along or you don't."

She nodded. Neither of us moved. I reached one arm behind me for my cocktail and sipped it. "You know, the garlic's gonna burn, you don't let go of me."

"Or you could turn the heat off and we could eat later."

It took a stern grip to hold on to my drink. As a gentleman, I did not want to appear too eager, so I set it down carefully. "I do think these ingredients will keep," I said speculatively. I set my drink down and lifted an eyebrow at her. I tried to summon one of the carefully managed smiles I put on while working.

I could never, ever control the kind of smile I showed her. I was sure I looked like an idiot, or a sled dog, or both.

She knocked back the rest of her own drink and stepped away, took me by the wrist.

I turned the heat off on the stove before we slipped through the hatch into my bunk.

* * *

Dinner wasn't served until nine, which was later than I liked to eat, but I was willing to make allowances for present company. It was good, and served the job of keeping everyone warm. Two bodies moving around inside my buttoned-up galley had warmed the small space up considerably and I was puttering around in just shorts and a t-shirt. Gen had put on an old orange sweatshirt of mine that had "ILLINOIS" across it in faded blue.

We ate quietly, sitting across from one another with our knees touching under my tiny table. For a long time, the only sound besides spoons and bowls—or the occasional tearing of a piece of bread, from her side of the table—was the quiet mix of music I'd turned on.

"So, next Saturday," she said, returning the last conversation we'd been having.

"Right. So…would you want to come?"

"What's on the menu?"

"It's Second Thanksgiving. But the best one I know how to cook, with the able assistance of any volunteers."

"And Dani invited me?"

"She and Emily were emphatic that I should bring you if you wanted to come."

"Well, I think I do."

"Good." I was lost for a moment. "Uh, do you want to come with me, or meet me there, or…"

She hadn't taken her eyes off me. She laughed a little. I think she enjoyed how flustered I got. I tugged at my shirt for lack of anything else to do.

"Why wouldn't I just come with you?"

"Well, I have to get there pretty early and I spend all morning and afternoon cooking."

"Well," she said, "I would like to help." She set her arms on the table and leaned slightly forward, over her empty bowl.

"Why that and not Thanksgiving Day, with your family? I know it's only been a couple of months," she was quick to add. "It just seems really important to you, but it's not, you know…the actual holiday."

"Ehh," I said, lifting a hand and giving it one of those back-and-forth shaking kind of gestures. "For me, and Dani, Second Thanksgiving is more of a holiday."

If I was ever going to let my parents—my dad—meet Gen, it was going to be under circumstances I could control a lot more easily than Thanksgiving Day.

"I get it," Gen said. "I can handle friends-giving. I would love to come," she said, sitting up straighter, jokingly formal. "Please tell Danielle I would be delighted to accept her invitation."

"I will. They're excited to meet you."

Her mouth twisted a little, and her eyes were suddenly shrewd. "How many girls have you *brought* to Second Thanksgiving?"

"You'd be the first." That was the true answer, and apparently the right one, since she stood up from her set, came around the table, and slid into my lap.

There was a kiss, then she laid her head on my chest.

The only sound on the deck was Townes Van Zandt's plaintive voice singing "Close Your Eyes, I'll be Here in The Morning."

Chapter 3

When Gen left early the next morning—she had flexible enough hours to get in to work a little late—she leaned against me and kissed my cheek and murmured.

"I like your boat, and I like that you are on it, but it's getting a little cold. See you tomorrow night."

She was right. It hadn't gotten any warmer since yesterday and riding It up Route 40 in another day of driving late fall rain did not have the same zing as it did yesterday. I couldn't decide if that was because I was no longer tailing someone.

That did feel like the real PI stuff. I just needed there to be an inheritance at stake, or perhaps a complicated ownership situation involving some high-priced art that the two parties were trying to keep from one another for it to feel really right.

But ultimately it had been about a husband getting a handjob from a woman who wasn't his wife in the front of an expensive car he'd just bought a month ago. It was midlife crisis bingo.

And now I had to go into the office and lay it out for an attorney and a wife and be a part of someone's family dissolving.

I liked my job. I hated my job. It was the only thing I could do, unless I wanted to go sling hash in a chain restaurant. And that would be far worse.

I pulled It in between two of my coworker's bland boxes and, as I thought of them that way, realized I was fighting a losing battle with the sneering biker mindset.

On into the offices of Dent-Clark Investigations I went. I'd been a little more common sight there lately; Jason had bugged me to come in to the office at least four times a week. I ignored him and made it two, and so far the unspoken compromise had worked.

I was used to attention in the office, since I was an uncommon sight, and also the only one who walked in wearing riding gear and carrying a helmet. But everyone's attention was focused on one of my coworkers who was standing in the middle of the room with his shirt half-off.

Brock Diamante was back in the office after a nearly two-month long convalescence, and he had scars to share and a story to tell.

He was bent over showing off the livid round scar that a biker's bullets had left in his shoulder. Bullets that had been meant for me. They were my fault, or at least partly my responsibility.

I sidled up and let him finish his moment.

"Mostly a clean through and through," he was saying, as he displayed his shoulder—tattooed bicep subtly flexed, not that subtlety was a big part of Brock. "Little bit of secondary infection but I heal fast. Ain't that some shit? A year in the Middle East and I never get a splinter. Home for a few months and I get shot."

People around him assured him that it was, in fact, some shit. The crowd broke up—though one of our coworkers, a woman named Karen, took a long and lingering look at Brock's arm as she went back to her desk.

"Brock," I said, sticking out a hand. "Good to see you up and around."

He took my hand and gave it a hard shake. "Jack. Hey, brother. Thanks for coming to see me in the hospital. And the MP3 player…I got a new phone now, so I can pay you back for that."

He'd kept pumping my hand the entire time. Being laid on his back for as long as Brock had been had taken something out of him, but he could still give a hand a hard squeeze.

Whether it was his moment in the spotlight or not, I wasn't going to give him the satisfaction of letting go first, so we went on pumping arms a while.

Then I realized I'd only gone to see him for the first week he'd been in there, and had completely let it slip my mind since.

"No need to pay me back for anything, Brock. I should've had your back. I owe you one."

"Then you'll bring me along on whatever you're doing next."

"What I'm doing next, mostly, involves going to court. You want to come along with me, fine…but it's not gonna be very exciting."

"I meant your next real case."

"Don't know what that'll be till I finish this one," I said.

"And it's time to get into the conference room and get on with it," boomed a voice from the manager's corridor.

Jason Clark, the managing partner of Dent-Clark Investigations, stood there in a dark brown houndstooth tweed, blue tweed waistcoat, and dark jeans. This was a casual look for him, and put together, it probably cost as much as my entire wardrobe. Rank has its privilege and pay grade is among them.

"Later, Brock," I said. I followed Jason into his office. At the conference table in it sat Mrs. Jackson and her lawyer. The former was a woman nearing fifty years old. She had glossy dark hair, cut short but clearly well taken care of, a dark green suit, simple but tasteful makeup. Her lawyer was probably my age, also a woman, taller than I was in the black heels she wore with her blue pinstripes.

"Mrs. Jackson, Ms. Hanes, this is Jack Dixon. He's been in the field on your behalf," Jason said. I shook hands with the both of them. I felt underdressed but a thermal Henley and jeans was basically my cold weather uniform unless I'd gotten specific instructions to dress otherwise.

I could smell coffee. In fact, I had smelled it from the main office, and not the burnt, acidic swill that was brewed by the gallon in the breakroom. The smell of the good stuff. Carefully roasted beans. French press. It was on Jason's sideboard.

"Can I get anyone coffee?" I put on the brightest voice and the most chipper smile I had—pretty low wattage, but eager to help—as I glided over to the sideboard.

"Two creams, no sugar," Jason said. Mrs. Jackson and her lawyer demurred. I poured two mugs, carefully emptying three yellow packets of sweetener into mine, and carried them over. The wronged wife and the lawyer sat at one end of the conference table; Jason and I sat along the sides, across from one another.

"So." Ms. Hanes took a leather portfolio from her briefcase and a fountain pen from a pocket. Given the fit and cut of her suit, the inlay on the pen, the fact that both briefcase and portfolio looked very much like real leather, I'd imagine her hourly rate was considerably north of mine.

Should've stayed in school.

"Can you describe Mr. Jackson's behavior while you observed him yesterday?"

"Picked up a woman at a park and ride. They headed west-bound on route 40 towards the Hatem Bridge and Havre de Grace. Slightly before then is when, at a stop light, I slipped the tracking device onto the bumper per the client's request."

"And how would you describe the behavior of Mr. Jackson with the woman?"

Jubilant. "I, uh, would call it…infidelity."

"You have visual confirmation of that?"

"I would say that, within a certain limited definition, yes. I do."

"And Mr. Clark, the firm stands ready to provide surveillance photographs."

"We do." Jason set a flash drive down on the table. "I can display some of them," he said, gesturing towards the pair of large screens that hung above his desk.

The lawyer looked to her client, who nodded.

Jason went to his desk and clicked the thumb drive into place. In moments, one of the screens began showing photos of Mr. Jackson and his companion—young, nubile, blonde—staggering into a roadside motel room. In his hand was a bottle of wine. His belt was hanging open before they got through the door.

"Time stamp has this at 2:33 p.m., yesterday afternoon. They left the motel at approximately 5:35," Jason said. "The motel's registry probably won't help us much unless he used his own name and a credit card…"

"Or hers," Mrs. Jackson said.

"We have not made any progress identifying the woman Mr. Jackson was seen with."

The meeting droned on like this. I made the appropriate noises when asked and tried not to make too much eye contact with Mrs. Jackson. She was holding up pretty well from what I could see, but I got the sense that she was a woman who was used to holding a tight lid on her expressions.

I tuned back in when I heard Jason saying something that ended with "…any further services the firm can provide?"

Mrs. Jackson suddenly pointed at me. "Can I hire him to toss my hus…to toss Donald around like a ragdoll?"

"That's a joke," the lawyer said firmly before I could even muster a chuckle.

Mrs. Jackson looked straight at me and mouthed *I'm not joking*. I pretended not to understand her.

"I think our business is about done," Ms. Hanes said. "Thank you, Mr. Clark and Mr. Dixon, for your professionalism *and* your discretion."

I glanced at Jason. "Do we have business cards that say that? You'll thank us for our professionalism *and* our discretion?"

Jason gave me the kind of forced chuckle that wasn't really laughter at all and I sipped my coffee in a vain attempt to hide my smile. He escorted Ms. Hanes out but Mrs. Jackson indicated that she wanted to stay behind to talk to me.

"I wasn't joking," she began in a whisper, but I waved her away.

"Mrs. Jackson…"

"Katherine."

"Katherine, I'm not for hire in that way."

"Five hundred dollars."

"I don't like violence, Mrs. Jackson. I don't like hurting people."

"A thousand."

"Could be a million, not going to change," I said, though I wasn't really entirely sure how much I meant that.

She heaved a sigh and went out after her lawyer, who would doubtless have been mortified to know that her client had just made a firm cash offer to have her husband beaten.

Jason exchanged end-of-case pleasantries, certainly slipping in a careful reminder about billing and payment. My phone buzzed in my pocket.

I saw the name of the sender and did a double-take. I clicked it open.

"Watch your office mail, bro! Sent you something. - Grant."

It had been sent from an alumni email address from the university I'd attended—and ignominiously left.

"Stop using your phone on company time," Jason said as he re-entered the room. I looked him in the eye for a moment and then re-read the email.

"I get any mail at the office lately?"

"You never get mail at the office. You haven't started sending bills here to avoid collection, have you?"

"I don't get any paper bills. That's nineteenth century stuff, paper transactions. As obsolete as black powder weapons."

"If I issued you a single-shot black powder pistol, would you carry that? Maybe a bandoleer of them? Would fit with your whole pirate thing."

"I am not a pirate, as I do not seize property or prizes on the seas, high or otherwise, and I resent the implication. If anything, I have participated in the longtime war of the forces of justice and right *against* piracy."

"Being a Navy cook and a short stint as a DNR cop don't make you Robert Maynard, Jack."

"Never said they did." I slid my phone into my pocket, finally. "What's next?"

Jason smiled broadly. "Paperwork. So much paperwork, as you close out all the details and expenses of this case."

"You know, I was thinking that until Brock can get back out in the field, shouldn't we just have him handling all the paperwork..."

He pointed to the door. "Finish the case file and close it out."

I knew more or less exactly how far I could push my boss on most days, and I was within sight of the limit. I got up and went to find an empty desk.

Chapter 4

I was two stoplights away from the office when I picked up my not-at-all-subtle tail, a dark blue Audi I recognized from just two days before.

I wasn't entirely sure how he'd known to follow me, but there was no question he was following me when, just to be sure, I blew through a yellow that had just gone red, and he actually pulled *around* another car to plow straight through the intersection.

Even that might have been coincidence—asshole drivers are everywhere—but for him leaning out of his window screaming obscenities at me. His face was bright red, a rictus of anger.

And he quickly made it apparent that he wasn't so much interested in *tailing* me as in *hitting* me, or at least running me off the road.

Now, I'm not much of a car guy. I don't know about horsepower or torque or acceleration beyond being aware that they exist and are important to some people. On a straightaway I'd bet that his shiny new Audi could outmuscle It any day.

But it wasn't a straightaway, there was traffic, and I had a much easier time of ducking between other vehicles than he did. I dove into a gap between two trucks and then around them on the shoulder and back on to the road.

I could hear him honking behind me, and the trucks honking

back. But I had one more stoplight, a left turn, and a winding road through an office park to the firm.

It was a good time to find out just what kind of speed I could coax out of It. Turned out to be plenty, and I was equal parts exhilarated and terrified when I slewed into the parking lot. I'd like to say I spun it around perfectly into a spot, but what I really did was come to a stop between rows of parked cars that almost threw me over the handlebars.

I got off the bike, but I left my helmet, gloves, and jacket on. I heard a tormented precision engine making its way up the drive. The Audi careered past the entrance to the firm. I heard brakes squeal and then the engine shut off then angry footsteps.

I sighed and slipped my helmet off. But I kept it clutched in one gloved hand as I walked to the entrance.

Donald Jackson, haggard, short of breath, was stomping like an angry rain cloud towards me. Once he registered me in his vision he let out an inarticulate noise of anger and charged, one fist upraised.

I had plenty of options. I was wearing Kevlar gloves; I could probably put him down with two-thirds of a punch. I could probably take the punch if it was aimed at my body, similarly Kevlared. I could have brought my helmet up to the side of his head and cracked his scalp wide open, but I had paid good money for the Blue Squadron X-Wing pilot customization and I wasn't taking any chances with it.

I could, if I had both hands free, have slipped the punch, taken his wrist and his elbow with my hands, and put his arm up behind his back in a classic come-along.

Heck, I probably could've just tripped him.

As it was, I waited until he was pot-committed and just sidestepped. He went swinging into empty air and overbalanced so far that he almost went down.

"That's a free one," I said. "You're lucky it didn't land."

"YOU," he yelled. "You ruined my marriage."

"You realize everyone who can hear you thinks that means I'm sleeping with your wife, right?"

He came at me again, arms outstretched, trying for a tackle. He had fifteen years on me, no wind, and no training. This was as unfair as a fight could be, and I had no real desire to hurt him.

But I decided just a little clarification of the facts would benefit both me and Mr. Jackson.

So I sidestepped again, but I threw my left boot out and tangled up his legs. He went down hard, hitting the asphalt with an *oomph* of lost breath.

"Are we done, or are you out to embarrass us both some more?"

"You ruined my marriage," he yelled again, as he started to push himself up. I thought, briefly, of planting a boot on the small of his back, but that was more contact than I really wanted to engage in.

"I think you probably did that, Donny," I said.

He found a burst of strength from somewhere and pushed up to his feet. This time I didn't step aside or trip him. I let him smack straight into me. I had my feet set, years of grappling training, heavy-tread boots, and an armored jacket. He had dress shoes, no ability to focus his body strength, and what smelled like a three-martini lunch on his breath.

There wasn't much of an impact. With my free hand, I caught his collar and tie and twisted them as hard as I could.

I had him, essentially, by the throat. And he quickly realized it. I pulled his face up close to mine.

"Couple of things, Donny," I began calmly. "First, I really don't appreciate you trying to run me down. Roads are hard enough for bikers as it is; I don't need an asshole like you making it that much harder."

He croaked something out. Couldn't tell if it was an apology or a complaint or a request for air. For the moment, I didn't much care. He wasn't in danger of passing out.

Yet.

"Second. You need to rethink this 'ruined my marriage' thing and *work on your goddamn character*. Infidelity followed closely by trying to kill the man your wife hired to investigate it are not the actions of a blameless man. Are we clear?"

His face was nearing purple. I heard some noise behind me; we'd probably attracted a crowd from the office. Donald Jackson's head bobbed quickly up and down.

I eased off the pressure on his collar, but I kept my grip on his tie. He began taking huge, heaving breaths. I was suddenly hit with a cloud of gin-and-feta-stuffed-olive breath.

"Thirdly," I said. "Gimme your damn car keys."

Tears popped into his eyes. He'd been found out, unmanned, and now he was going to cry.

"You can't take my car, man, I just bought that, I put ten grand down…"

"I don't *want your fucking car*."

The tears halted. He sniffled. Behind us, the crowd stopped tittering. I was not known as much of a shouter, but I had just gotten loud.

It was the way Donald Jackson had whipsawed through the least attractive emotions of his range. His anger, his determination to lash out at me, the way he was blaming someone else for his own faults, when what he was really angry about was getting caught. Then crying, not because he'd laid himself bare and looked with horror at what he'd found.

But because he thought I wanted his car. What I *wanted* was to give him a good shaking.

"I don't give a shit about your car. I don't want you back on the road because you are obviously drunk. Give me your goddamned keys." He gingerly fished them out of a jacket pocket and held them out. I let go of his collar and snatched them away.

"Walk to the nearest gas station. It's about four blocks that way," I said, pointing. "Get some coffee. In an hour, you come back and you seem sober, you can have these back."

"What...I don't..." He looked like he wanted to reopen discussions. I didn't.

I seized his tie again and tugged, lifting him to his tiptoes.

Behind me, I heard Jason's voice.

"Put him down, Jack."

I did what my boss told me to. The calming tone of his voice helped.

"Go," I said. "You can have the keys back when you're sober."

Sheepishly he started away, head sunk low.

I tucked the keys in my jacket pocket and stalked into the office.

Chapter 5

Once inside, I headed straight for a bathroom and locked the door behind me. I took off my Kevlar gloves and set them on a sink, then bent down to splash water on my face.

My hands shook, but only a little. Adrenaline was still surging through me, making me jittery and angry. I took a few deep breaths, stared hard at myself in the mirror.

"Need to trim your beard," I said to my reflection. I tended to let it grow out, but Gen had expressed an admiration—not necessarily a preference—for the short trim I'd gotten just before our first date.

I took a couple more handfuls of water and splashed them into my eyes and top of my head. Then I picked up my gloves and went back into the office.

Jason waved me to his door and shut it behind him.

"Coffee?"

"Don't think I need anything to jangle my nerves any more than they already are," I answered.

"Let me rephrase," Jason said, opening a drawer in his desk and coming up with a bottle of Wigle organic corn bourbon. "Coffee?"

"Sure."

He retrieved a couple of mugs from the sideboard where his coffee supplies resided. He sat back down, uncorked the bottle, and poured careful measures into each. We clinked mugs.

I took a sip. I didn't drink this early in the day, as a rule. But the smooth sweet corn notes of the bourbon was just the thing for the anger that kept ticking over in me.

"What was that about?"

"Asshole followed me. And by 'followed' I mean 'tried to run me off the goddamned road.'"

"I wonder how he spotted you," Jason said, with a slight grin.

I eyed him over the rim of the mug. I was drinking his bourbon so I couldn't afford to get too smart in reply.

"Could it possibly be the helmet."

"I paid good money for this helmet."

"I don't doubt that you did, but there aren't *too many* of those."

"Hey." I set the helmet on my lap, tapping the green side. "For what I paid for this Blue Squadron paintjob, you better not see *any* others."

We shared a laugh and both sipped more bourbon.

"So," my boss said, as he leaned back in his chair, "how many people is that trying to kill you in the last couple of months?"

"How many do the Aesir count as?"

"Too many," he said. His smile had vanished and his face had gone a little grim, like he was studying me, or adding up some things only he could see. Then he took a letter off his desk and handed it over to me.

It was addressed to me, care of the firm, in careful, if not especially neat, handwriting. Where the return address would be, there was a large logo in three big, blocky letters: DWF. Underneath that, it read Delmarva Wrestling Federation.

"Delmarva wrestling?" I looked at Jason, and he shrugged, then handed me an opener shaped like a Civil War cavalry saber. I cut the envelope open. A letter wrapped around a pair of smaller pieces of paper tumbled out.

I took a look at the letter.

Jack,

Heard you were back in this area. I'm in a show on the Wilmington Riverfront this weekend. Thought you might like to come by and watch, maybe catch up. Hope to see you there,

Grant

One of the smaller pieces of paper was a ticket with this Saturday's date and RIVERFRONT RUMBLE on it. The other was an all access pass, the kind meant to be slipped into a plastic sleeve and worn on a lanyard. It had my name and "Comp/Talent" with initials GA on it—standing for, I presumed, Grant Aronson. I hadn't thought about him, or any of the rest of my college wrestling teammates, since the day I'd walked off campus and found myself at an enlistment center. I was so lost thinking about it—bus rides, plane rides, meets, training, sweating, being miserable more or less twenty-four hours a day—that I didn't hear Jason until he called my name twice. I finally looked up, blinking away college memories.

"Yeah?"

"So what's all this about?"

I looked up at him. "I guess one of my old college teammates is, uh…still in the wrestling game. Sort of."

"Sort of?"

I held out the letter and he took it and glanced over it.

"Delmarva Wrestling Federation?" If anything, he was more puzzled than I was.

"Professional wrestling," I said.

"The fake kind."

"I wouldn't call it that around the folks who do it," I said. "Not unless you want an earful. At the least."

He shrugged. "Why's this guy reaching out?"

"Don't know. We were friends as teammates, I guess. But that was almost ten years ago now. We don't talk a lot. Facebook friends. That kind of thing."

Jason lowered his head and looked at me over the rim of his spectacles. "*You* have Facebook."

"It's a useful investigative tool."

"I know that, but you can use a dummy account for that." He tapped his lip with one finger. "Is it mostly artful pictures of cocktails on the deck of your boat in the sunset?"

"It is *sometimes* that."

"Oh ho. And what else? Pictures of carefully staged plates?"

This was getting a little much. "I eat almost all of my dinners out of a jar," I said, and I could feel some heat creeping into my cheeks. "Can I have that back now?" He set it down on the desk.

"Speaking of dinner, you owe me one, remember? We made a bet on the Kennelly kid."

"Right." I stood up, pulled out my wallet, and dropped three twenties and a ten on his desk. "There. That'll cover you for Prost. Enjoy."

I snatched the letter off his desk and wrapped it back around the ticket and the backstage pass as I walked out of his office. Behind me I heard him sputtering some kind of uncertainty or apology, but I didn't care. I tucked the letter into the interior pocket of my jacket and went straight out the door. I wanted to climb back on to It and ride straight back to the *Belle*. I could see the afternoon and evening stretch out before me. Going from one book to another, reading a few pages before setting it down. Pacing, not that a thirty-four-foot houseboat offers a lot of room for that. You've got to be prepared to make a lot of turns. Then eventually making a cocktail that would turn sour with anger in my mouth.

It was going to be a classic evening at home alone, is what I was thinking.

Then I felt Mr. Jackson's keys in my pocket and realized that I would, in fact, be committing grand theft auto, more or less, if I sped away. I was not necessarily opposed to treading on the rules when I needed to but major felonies were a bit out of my line.

So I paced in the parking lot for a few minutes, then sheepishly went back into the office, took as isolated a cubicle as I could find, and sat down. I made sure the Jackson file was completely closed, though I also added in a note about her husband's attack. Needed to be documented in case any of us got involved in the divorce proceedings.

Then I started flipping through old case files I'd worked on to see if there was anything interesting in them. There wasn't. Just a litany of broken promises, cheating partners and spouses, lying employees, lying bosses, the usual.

I got the letter and tickets back out and decided to check out the Delmarva Wrestling Federation. Their website was slickly made and contemporary looking, which I didn't expect, but the instant I opened it the speakers on the computer I was on began blaring heavy metal. Startled, I knocked the mouse clear off the desk and fumbled with the keyboard for a few moments before I got the damn thing muted.

Red-faced, I grabbed the mouse off the floor and slunk down in the chair, hoping no one had noticed.

It looked like a pretty standard wrestling company, I guess. Good guys, bad guys, lots of music, chanting crowds, arenas that looked full, if a bit on the smaller side. I'd had my pro wrestling phase as a kid but had moved on once I discovered combat sports like boxing and mixed martial arts. I assumed everyone else had moved on as well, but that wasn't the case. Grant had followed the stuff well into college and, obviously, beyond. I remember him trying to tell me about the terminology, but I didn't remember any of it. He recorded any of the weekly shows he missed when the team traveled, obsessively read wrestling blogs, and had a collection of old shows on his computer, on DVD, even on VHS.

On the website's roster, I couldn't find "Grant Aronson," but I did find "U.S. Grant," and there he was, my old teammate. Instead of the orange and blue wrestling singlets and headgear I remembered him in, he was wearing star-spangled blue trunks and boots, a Civil War-era black cavalry trooper's hat—I thought so, anyway, I'm not any kind of expert—and a black vest.

Grant had been the kind of cornfed, all-for-the-team guy I'd encountered a lot in my wrestling career. They took every motivational slogan every coach gave them and stirred it into a fiery slurry in their mind that made them good wrestlers, perfect teammates, and excellent partiers—but strictly in the off-season.

Sometime around age sixteen, I had stopped being one of those guys. Convinced I was smarter than them, I had taken every word a coach said that didn't directly pertain to technique or training and discarded it as misguided advice at best, open psychological warfare at worst. I spent the bus trips to meets reading fantasy novels—or, worse, the books that were a part of my philosophy major—and ignoring everyone else. I had looked on coaches and teammates alike with a mix of pity and scorn, secure in my superiority.

And yet there Grant was, smiling widely, traveling the country— or at least the mid-Atlantic and the south—doing something that he seemed to love. Here I was, stuck in an office, waiting for an afternoon drunk to come get his keys. He'd finished his college education with, presumably, his degree in communications, psychology, or exercise science. Those are what I remembered every teammate majoring in.

I had two years worth of credits towards a philosophy degree that had probably expired. Who was actually the smart one here?

He had the same crew-cut blond hair, blue eyes, and bluff Scandinavian features that girls in college had loved. If his cheekbones were a little more prominent, his neck thicker, his skull a little wider than I remembered, well, that wasn't *necessarily* the work of PEDs. I wasn't in any place to judge anybody's personal use of pharmaceuticals, not really. Not with a reminder to call Eddie pinging around my brain.

I couldn't tell from the website what Grant's role was, whether he was a good guy or a villain or just a fill-in, but there was a lot of info. He was billed as from Point Pleasant, Ohio—which a quick dip into Wikipedia confirmed was the real Ulysses S. Grant's birthplace— though I knew he was damn sure from Indiana. It had a list of his signature moves, none of which made any sense to me. There were some embedded video clips of moves, and one of him giving an interview. I didn't quite have it in me to click on them just now. Besides, it was about time for Donald Jackson to come looking for his keys, so I wandered back outside.

I found him lurking around the edge of the parking lot, a large Wawa coffee cup in one hand and a pastry bag in the other. He set the coffee down, pulled a chocolate chip muffin out of the bag, and took a huge bite.

I felt a surge of overwhelming hunger as I sidled up to him. He devoured the thing in three or four messy bites. A scattering of crumbs and chocolate smears around the sides of his mouth were the only remaining evidence of its existence by the time he saw me.

"Gimme my keys back," he said. I stared at him. He picked up the pastry bag and held it out as though it might appease me. "Pumpkin spice. Can't resist that seasonal stuff, you know?" He let out a weak chuckle. "Want it?" I said nothing, still, watching him with what I'd describe as a zoo-goer's curiosity.

I stared at him till he lowered the bag, shrugged, pulled out a second muffin, and ate it. Finally I pulled out his keys.

"I hope that a walk, a coffee, and fourteen hundred calories worth of sugar has sobered you up enough to drive," I said as I held them out.

He took them tentatively. "Who counts calories?"

I had done it for so long I hadn't even needed to look up what those muffins weighed in at, but I didn't see the need to unburden myself to a drunken philanderer.

Donald Jackson was the kind of asshole who apparently could not abide silence.

"Well, whatever, I took a walk, it balances out."

"That's not how that works," I said. "And you'd have to walk ten or twelve miles to burn off the calories you just ate, even if it did. You're not really big on accountability or self discipline, are you?"

"What the hell kind of question is that?"

"Look," I said, waving a hand at him, "I shouldn't even be talking to you. Get the hell out of here—but I swear to God if you're still drunk and cause an accident on the way home because of it, and hurt anyone other than yourself, I'll..." I stopped myself from finishing the sentence. Directly voicing threats was a bad move, especially since I had been employed by his wife. I quickly switched gears.

"How'd you know to look for me, anyway?"

"My wife told me you were the guy who tailed me...put a tracker on my car, said I could find you here. That car tracking shit ain't even legal..."

That's what he said. What I heard was, *My wife tried to set me up for the ass-kicking she had thought she could purchase.*

"Your wife's name is on the car registry. She owns it the same as you. Means she can track it if she wants to." And judging from the way things were developing, my guess is she would own the car entirely by herself in a few months.

He snorted and stalked away. "You're easy to find with that dumb Star Wars helmet. Nerd."

That was his big parting shot. As he walked away, having been humiliated, to the overpriced car he didn't know how to drive, probably to go see the girlfriend who was going to cost him the ability to afford that. I rode a motorcycle I owned free and clear. But somehow I was the nerd.

I sighed, went back into the office, and made the executive decision to skip lunch so that I could stop at Capriotti's and get a sub for dinner.

Chapter 6

I could only occasionally glimpse the appeal of living on dry land. Saturday morning at eight a.m. in Gen's apartment was one of those times. It was warm, no one was banging around on the docks outside, and it wasn't swaying with the river.

In fact the last bit was probably why I'd been awake more or less since six-thirty. I had long since distanced myself from the rigorous scheduling of the Navy, but I had kept the habit of being able to sleep more or less whenever I could. That didn't seem to be working just now and I could only attribute it to the lack of motion.

I didn't mind. Gen was sleeping with her back to me, and it was a nice back, toned and glowing with health. I could see the black lines of the tattoo on her right bicep—clean linework of an anthropomorphized mouse wearing a sunhat, carrying a map and with an old-fashioned flash-bulb camera around her neck. My staring must've woken her because she rolled over to face me.

She put one hand n my shoulder and pushed me onto my back, then levered her head onto my opposite shoulder. Her hand moved over the one and only tattoo I had, on my right pec.

"When did you get this?"

"While I was in the Navy. Early on."

"No anchors? Ship names? Just a tree?"

"Well. Not a tree, the tree. Of Gondor."

Her fingers moved over the script written beneath it. "Been a long time since I saw those movies. Or read the books," she added. "You're not the only one who reads," as if she was heading off any mention on my part of the books' existence. "And you got the words at the same time?"

"Yeah. I don't think they get said in the movies."

She leaned over me, peered down at my chest. "I do not wish for such triumphs," she said. "Who says that?"

"Faramir," I said, and I only just stopped myself from elaborating on the differences in his character from book to film.

"What's it mean?"

"For me or him?"

"I'm not dating him."

"I'm not really sure anymore. It was about leaving behind wrestling, I guess. And not seeking out any kind of combat arms job when I signed up."

"Did they want you to?"

"Recruiters all wanted me to at least try it, 'cause of the shape I was in, I guess. Division I college wrestler in the middle of his season. I was lucky none of them were college wrestling fans, they didn't try to talk me out of it. Boot camp was not much of a challenge."

"Why'd you pick the Navy?"

"I was already in the area I'd go for training. It was the one I could start the soonest, and it meant I didn't have to come back home."

She settled back down onto my shoulder but kept her hand on my chest. Her words were muffled, and the way her mouth moved against my chest tickled. I didn't mind.

"You were good?"

"As a cook or a wrestler?"

"Wrestler."

"Yep."

"Not going to elaborate?"

"There's not much to elaborate on. I was good, from high school on. I started hearing from recruiters and coaches after my sophomore year."

"And you really walked away from paid-for college right in the middle of it?"

"Yep."

"Why?"

I shook my head, took a slightly deeper breath. "Just...walked away," I said, a bit of a white lie, also a bit of the truth. "I didn't want to do it anymore. Couldn't do it anymore. I never really liked it anyway, and when I got to college they wanted me to wrestle at one-eighty-four."

"Pounds?" She lifted her head up, eyebrows knitted together in confusion.

"Yep."

"That's a little skinny for you, isn't it?"

"Well, I certainly thought so, but that didn't stop them from pushing me that way. I argued to move up but they always assumed they knew what was best."

"Did you like the Navy better?"

"Not really, but I liked not having my room and board depending on starving myself and working out all the time. I liked having a job that I got paid for. I guess I liked the idea that I was learning a trade."

She nodded along, stifled a yawn, and rubbed her head on my shoulder till she found a more comfortable spot. "Anywhere you have to be today?"

"Maybe?"

"Why maybe?"

I sighed. "Funny you should have asked about wrestling...one of my old teammates is in town. With a wrestling promotion, of all things. You know, the pro stuff..."

She leaned up. "What promotion?"

"Uh, Delmarva Wrestling Federation?"

"My dad loves pro wrestling. I used to watch it with him when I was a kid."

"You want me to call and see if I could get extra tickets? He gave me one, plus a backstage pass. I could probably get a couple more."

"Could you?"

"Sure. Let me just get my phone."

Gen bounced out of bed and went to put coffee on. I looked on my phone for the email Grant had sent me. There was no phone number associated, but I mailed back a quick request: Could I bring two more people to the show?

To my surprise, by the time I was sitting in Gen's kitchen with a cup of coffee, I'd already gotten a reply.

Absolutely. Tickets probably won't be all seated together. And I really need you to come backstage. Might have work for you. - Grant.

It suddenly dawned on me that I was going to be seeing a teammate I hadn't seen since I'd walked out on college, meeting Gen's dad, and trying to work all at once. It was going to be a complicated Saturday night.

Chapter 7

The afternoon became a flurry of activity. I had to ride back to the *Belle* to change clothes, to the firm to get some intake paperwork in case Grant was serious about hiring me, and ride back up to Delaware. Thankfully the rain had abated but it was still a cold day spent riding, rather than shut away in Gen's Wilmington apartment like I had hoped.

There were also text messages from my boss, telling me to take a weapon, that I ignored. For all I knew, Grant—or the company—wanted me to find a lost dog, check if a partner was cheating, or do a background check on someone.

It was also possible they wanted me to stand around looking severe and handsome, which I supposed I could also do. Finally, after the third text message imploring me to take some kind of weapon, a ship that had already sailed as the firm and its weapons lockers were far behind me, I listed these reasons to Jason, while pausing in my hasty lunch of an apple, a carrot, and three tablespoons of protein-enhanced almond butter.

Isn't there an outlaw biker gang that has a mark out on you?

Well, that part was true. I suddenly felt the lack of a holster on my belt. But then, it had been two months, a few members were in custody, and others were dead in the woods somewhere, done in by the locals who resented their encroachment.

In the weeks since I'd witnessed some local boys carry out the rural Maryland version of a gangland execution, I'd started to relax a bit.

I stopped doing that all at once. My shoulders began to itch as I remembered crime scene photos of a man who was probably one of those local boys with ribs cut out and his lungs pulled out over his back.

The Blood Eagle of Viking sagas brought to the twenty-first century. Though not eager to be their next practice case, I couldn't exactly tell my boss that. I needed to show him confidence, even if I had to do a better job of keeping my guard up.

Been two months. Haven't heard a peep. They've either moved on or been put to bed.

I got no reply, which meant he'd let it go. Then I got back on the road. The entire way back up to Wilmington, I kept a sharp eye out for other bikes. I felt a little itch in the middle of my back every time I saw or heard one, though none of the riders I saw were wearing a cut, much less any Aesir symbols.

* * *

I was back up in the trendy part of Wilmington an hour before the tickets said the doors would open to touch base with Gen and meet her dad. I parked It a few blocks away from her place because I wasn't sure that announcing my arrival with the rumble of a motorcycle's engine was really a winning play. I slipped off my gloves and helmet and stopped to adjust my jacket and my shirt at least half a dozen times before I made it into her building and knocked at the door.

She opened it, having changed into a dark t-shirt and black jeans that were tight enough to show off some of the muscle-tone of her legs, tucked into calf boots. She'd put on subtle makeup and just swept her hair back and tucked a simple brown woven band atop her head to keep it in place. I had yet to see Geneva Lawton wear something that didn't look great on her. I was interested to see how long that trend could continue. I was willing to bet it was an enduring character trait.

She took my hand, smiling, winked, but didn't lean up to kiss me as she might usually have. She led me into her apartment as her dad was levering himself up from a recliner.

He was a big barrel chested guy—not as tall as me, but not short. Big thick arms and neck, the kind that didn't have the tone of training, but had plenty of mass from a life of hard work. He had the kind of sun-browned skin that a person gets when their work and their leisure are all outside and probably near the water and they just don't have the time for a whole lot of sunscreen. He wore a black t-shirt with a faded deco of a bunch of big-name wrestlers of the 1980s, gray cargo shorts, and boots. He was apparently the kind of man who wore shorts unless it was actually snowing.

He shook my hand, firmly, but not in a way that was asking any questions about dominance. His hand was calloused and hard and quite frankly I wasn't sure who would've won a grip contest. I was just as happy not to find out.

"It's nice to meet you, Mr. Lawton," I said. "I'm Jack."

"Call me Bill," he said, "Mr. Lawton was my grandad." He had a graying handlebar mustache that had once been blond and a fringe of similarly colored hair around the sides of his head. "Thanks for bringing me along," he said. "Appreciate it."

"No problem," I said, then I stood there awkwardly with helmet and gloves in hands for a moment. "Gen tells me you're a big wrestling fan."

"Always was," he said. "Used to go down to Baltimore or up to Philly when the big shows came to town. Not so much these days since Genny don't want to come with me anymore," he said, teasing her, grinning.

She came up to his side and wrapped her arms around one of his. "Well, we can make up for it tonight," she said.

"Right," he said. Then he pointed at the helmet I was holding. "What do you ride?"

"Indian Scout," I said. "Twenty-fifteen."

He nodded lightly. "We'll take my truck to the show," he said. It was not phrased as a question. Gen smiled at me. While it was possible I might need to stay later than they wanted to if there was anything to Grant wanting to hire me, I didn't think that would be a particularly good argument to pick.

"Of course," I said with a grin. "No sense taking more than one car over." I set the helmet and the gloves down on a table and out the door we went.

Chapter 8

Bill's truck turned out to be one of those semi-extended cab types that pretended to have a backseat but didn't, really. Gen insisted I take shotgun next to her dad. On the one hand, I wouldn't have enjoyed cramming myself into the back for even a short trip. On the other hand, I was still meeting a girl's dad for the first time in more years than I cared to think about, and sitting next to him for a drive was not doing my nerves any good. At least it ought to be a short ride. It was a slow walk out to the truck, though; Mr. Lawton moved with the kind of hunched, slow gait that indicated a life spent bent over, with a shovel or a tool in hand.

"So," he began, once he'd levered himself into the truck and started it, "Genny tells me you're a private detective."

"Yes, sir," I agreed.

"That like bein' a cop for hire?"

"Uh, some people would think so, but I don't."

"Hrm. Is it like the movies?"

I had no idea what movies he meant. It could've been anything from *The Big Sleep* to *The Big Lebowski*. Regardless, there was a safe answer.

"Not really sir, no."

Another considered *hrm*. "Why don't be a cop, then?"

"I was," I said. "Just for a couple of years."

"Where at? Cecil County?"

"Well, technically all over Maryland. The waterways, anyway. I was Marine Police with the DNR."

"Damn, boy, you had a job where you got to ride around in a fast little boat all summer and you didn't keep it?"

Well, Mr. Lawton was certainly familiar with at least the more visible operations of DNR Police. In truth, that was probably the best and most sought-after part of the job. But it wasn't one I often did. Every cop does paperwork. Every cop answers phones. I had done too much of that.

"That much structure and scheduling wasn't really for me that soon after the Navy, sir."

"Ahh, you're a veteran, too. How many careers you had, Jack?"

"Three I guess, sir."

"Well, are you stickin' with this one?"

"Plan to, sir. It seems to be the right meeting of things I can do well and people who can stand me."

He reached out and poked my arm with one thick finger. It was like being jabbed with a fireplace poker. "Road crews always need a big fella like you, you ever looking for extra work. Don't have any full-time money just now but we're always hirin' part-timers. Good hourly money. Could be $20 an hour after a couplea months."

"I, uh, have a pretty good hourly rate at Dent-Clark, sir."

"How much?"

I told him. "Plus expenses."

He whistled low. "Nevermind then. You keep doing this private stuff. So long as you ain't getting shot at, anyway."

"It's really not like the movies that way, sir."

"I told you to call me Bill."

By then we were at the Riverfront, but a line of cars snaked from light to light.

"So, who's this friend of yours got the tickets?"

"Grant Aronson. I wrestled with him in college."

"You mean a different kind of wrestling, yeah?"

"Collegiate wrestling in the USA is mostly like freestyle wrestling," I said. "Which is one of the Olympic kinds. Not like the professional stuff at all."

"You go to the Olympics?"

"No."

"Could've?"

There was a question I didn't really want to answer. I resettled in my seat, and some look on my face must've spurred Gen into action. She leaned forward between the seats and put a hand on my arm, squeezing.

"That's probably enough for now, Dad," she said. "What's your friend's wrestling name?"

"Uh, U.S. Grant."

Her dad laughed. "Oh, he's an up-and-comer, alright. A heel."

"A…what?"

"Heel," Gen repeated for him. "A bad guy. A good guy is a babyface, or a face."

"Why would U.S. Grant be a bad guy," I wondered aloud, before I could stop myself.

"Think of the audiences," Gen muttered, just loud enough for me to hear, before slipping back into her seat.

"Bein' a heel don't mean the audience don't like him," Bill explained. "When the heel is good at what he does, you just…kinda get caught up in it, ya know? Like you would any movie."

I really didn't. But I was schooling myself not to judge, not only because this could be a job opportunity, but because Gen seemed to enjoy it enough to be up on the terminology.

I glanced to the backseat and grinned at her. I couldn't summon any of my working smiles around her. Not anymore. It was just a normal stupid, dumb-dog-looking grin. One I couldn't really control or manipulate like I could if I were approaching someone while on the clock. It can't have been handsome, or even charming.

She smiled back.

Goddamn.

Chapter 9

There were various lines outside the convention center snaking through metal barriers. I only had the one paper ticket; the other two were just so much digital information on my phone.

But I did have that backstage pass, and the first worker I showed it to ushered us straight past the line and into the building. Posters were up on wooden stands inside the lobby advertising various wrestlers with the promotion.

There was a Derrick Rigg—a mustachioed guy wearing a sharp gray suit that looked twenty years out of style, a loud black and gold striped tie, carrying a briefcase cuffed to his arm, and silver-mirrored-aviators. There was a man wearing a martial-arts gi that obscured his features, billed only as The Ninja. The third major billing went to a woman wearing what looked like mechanic's coveralls, with a wrench on her shoulder: Spitfire. I saw U.S. Grant in a list of names underneath her poster, but no headlines for him. I saw something about a ladder match and a weapons match and I hadn't the faintest idea what either of those could mean.

I was definitely on uncertain ground. On the other hand, Gen and her dad seemed right at home. "Heard about this girl," he was saying, pointing at the Spitfire poster. "Real high-flyin' stuff."

I looked at Gen. "Means she does aerial stuff, off the top ropes, or higher than that. Acrobatics."

"Huh. Well, the name would make sense, then."

Soon enough I found someone readily identifiable as security staff. He was as big as I was, with huge arms stuffed into a black polo shirt that was at least two sizes too small, and he had a headset on and a clipboard in his hands.

I walked over to him and pulled out the pass.

"My name's Jack Dixon. I was invited here by, uh…U.S. Grant? I've got my ID if you need it."

He held up one finger and went to his clipboard, spoke a few words I didn't catch into his headset, then looked up at me. "You can come back," he said. Then he pointed at Gen and her dad. "They can't."

I looked at Gen, and then at the security man. "We sure about that?"

"You're the only one gate listed," he said. "And I don't have time to vet anyone else, not when we're forty minutes from showtime."

Gen sidled up next to me and squeezed my arm.

"Go," she said. "It's work. We'll be fine."

"Have fun," I said.

"We will," she said, then kissed me on the cheek. I watched until she disappeared into the crowd with her dad.

I followed the security guy back past the front-facing, customer-oriented parts of the convention center. Every event space of any size has a network of tunnels and warrens a Tolkien Dwarf would feel right at home in, I've found. No sun, no signs indicating where to go. You either need to know the ground or have the unerring instinct of a born stage manager, security guard, or grifter. The latter helped because usually, somewhere in this kind of space, there are rooms full of food, booze, and possibly drugs. I've known people who could find all three from the center of a labyrinth with a blindfold on.

The security guard did not take long to dump me off on someone else, similarly holding a clipboard and wearing a headset, but much more in the 'backstage manager' than security vein. He also wore a black polo with the company label, and it was similarly two sizes too small, but it wasn't deliberately tight over the arms and chest so much as around the middle.

"Glenn," he said by way of introduction. His hand was sweaty, but I wouldn't have expected otherwise, since he was sweating from his ponytail to the back of his shirt. "Follow me."

Glen made pretty fast time. I had to stride quickly to keep up. He led me to a door, knocking and opening it one swift, practiced motion.

Looked like a green room, I supposed, not that I knew from green rooms. There was a table set with snacks, another long table with drinks from bottled water and energy drinks to beer, and a huge plastic bowl full of ice.

There were one or two other folks milling around in it. None of them were Grant. None of them looked like wrestlers.

"Uh, I'm here to see Grant Aronson," I said.

"Yep. He'll be along," Glen said, trying to head for the door.

"Uh, maybe you could take me to him?"

Glen shook his head. "Nope. He's in the clubhouse. Nobody in there but talent. *Nobody.*"

"Fine," I said. I found a bottle of water and started exploring the snacks. A bowl of waxy looking fruit; bowls of pretzels and chips that offered a seductive salt-and-carb high. The very thought of entering them into my calorie counting app was enough to move on.

Trays of limp, somewhat shiny lunchmeat, and a tray full of those slightly greasy, springy cubes of cheese.

It was the kind of catering one paid for by the foot. I studiously avoided it, thinking longingly of the carefully curated selection of nut butters in my galley on the *Belle*.

I didn't try and make any small talk with the other folks in the room, who looked like family or special guests. It wasn't hard; people tended not to approach me on their own.

The door swung open and in came Grant Aaronson, wearing his

ring gear—the black cavalry hat, the vest, the star-spangled trunks. Spurs jingled on the edge of his boots.

"Jack!" He threw his arms wide to hug me. I was less than enthusiastic about this because his mostly bare chest seemed to glisten with some kind of oil. And it wasn't as if we'd been all that close.

I was able to intercept his hand and turn it into one of those half-handshake half-hug things. I definitely felt a slick of moisture against my shirt and jacket, though.

"Long time no see, man," he boomed.

"Yeah. It's been, what…eight years? Thereabouts."

"Yeah, ever since the meet with…"

I waved him off. "Why'd you call me here, Grant?" I tried searching his face for any giveaway details, but he was wearing stage makeup and his eyes seemed a bit distant. I didn't really suspect drugs for that; before any kind of high-stress appearance before a crowd, it wasn't all that unusual for someone to seem distant. They might've been focusing, or psyching themselves up, or just glazing over at the thought of all the pressure. I'd never known Grant to be the worrying kind, though.

"Well, we can talk about that after the show, okay? I go on early, doing a quick undercard with Blake," he said, as if I knew who that was or what that meant.

"Can you at least thumbnail it for me?"

Grant cast his eyes around the room, clamped one hand around my wrist like a vise, and dragged me to a corner, distant from both the catering fand the occupants of the erstwhile VIP Lounge.

"There's threats against me, okay? Because of my character. Company doesn't want to go to the cops, so…I suggested you. Tell you more later!" He slapped me on the shoulder and vanished out the door.

In the small crowd in the green room I heard someone say, "Man, I hate that guy."

I looked. It was a kid, maybe fourteen, wearing a shirt with the Confederate flag that said "If this offends you, you need a history lesson."

I figured I could probably scrub that kid from the suspect list, but I gave him a hard stare until he paled and turned back to his mom.

Chapter 10

I didn't really want to test my willpower against the craft-services-by-the-yard table any longer than I had to. Even the worst, most grease-oozing cube of bad cheddar starts to look tempting after a long enough time spent staring at it.

So with my lanyard around my neck, I looked around for another stage hand or manager type who might direct me somewhere more useful, where I might be able to see the show and get a sense of why Grant might be incurring threats. Though I think I had an idea.

I found Glen rushing by and gently pulled him aside. "There somewhere I can watch the show?"

"You got a ticket, don't you?"

He had a point. I almost asked if he would show me back to the audience side of things but he had that frazzled look everyone who works in that sort of thing gets just as an event is starting. The kind that says, *If I get one more request, I will kill the person who makes it, or myself, or possibly both.*

I decided not to see if I was poor Glen's tipping point and went exploring myself. In a few moments I passed the 'clubhouse,' which looked like the largest back room available turned into a de facto dressing room. A black polo-shirted security man stood outside, giving me a hard stare as I walked by. I grinned at him.

Soon enough I was back past the ropes and into the late-arriving crowd. To my surprise, my seats proved to be ringside—not even the permanent seats from the venue, but a folding chair set up just a couple of yards away from the ring itself. I could feel the heat of the lights, smell the scent of it rising off the canvas, see the small scattering of chalk dust tossed across it.

I had very little idea what to expect, and so I craned my neck around the building, looking at the crowd. It seemed like a fairly full house—in vain I looked as if I might see Gen and her dad, but I had no idea where their seats even were.

Suddenly I was startled by the blare of music, and then a pre-recorded announcer voice, welcoming everyone to DELMARVA. WRESTLING.

A sector of the crowd cheered along with the name, then a louder cheer went up as someone in a tuxedo came strolling in from backstage, down a long corridor blocked off with movable metal gates.

My first surprise was that it was a woman wearing the tuxedo. The second was that, damn, she was indeed *wearing* that tuxedo. The spotlights that fell on her and the stage makeup she wore made it hard to guess her age, and it might just have been rude to do that anyway. North of mine, for sure, but she was giving the years every bit of fight they could handle. She had dark hair falling down her back, neatly waved at the end. She carried a mic in one hand and a cane that she twirled in the other. At each of her hands, and a half-step behind her, walked two men, both wearing trunks, ring-boots, and nothing else. They looked awfully similar—but that could've been the distance, the crew-cuts, and the matching oiled six-packs.

When she neared the ring the two fellows jumped into action. One of them hopped up ringside and pulled the ropes apart. The other went to one knee and made a basket with his hands. The tuxedoed woman put one shoe in his hand, stepped the other onto his shoulder, and gracefully passed under the held open ropes. Then the escorts hopped in behind her. The same active segment of the crowd had begun a chant.

"Daphne, Daphne, Daphne…" It would be hard to call it thunderous but there was no doubt it was loud. She acknowledged the cheers by raising her cane, once to each side of the ring. Then, with a dramatic sweep of it, the crowd fell immediately silent. She raised the mic.

"Good evening, Wilmington." Somehow the woman managed to purr and exclaim into the mic at the same time. I was impressed all over again.

"Who is ready to see the gladiators of the modern day?" A cheer. "Who is ready for high-flying, death-defying, acrobatic grace?" A louder cheer. "And who is ready for some old. Fashioned. BRAWLING?"

Roars. People behind me stood up. A chant of her name broke out again; once more, she silenced it with another flourish of her cane.

"Remember, in the DWF, *you* choose each night's best performer! Be sure to get your ballots from the ushers, or the stations near the concessions! Results will be posted tomorrow, and the winner receives a bonus. Because in Delmarva, the FAN'S voice matters!"

I wondered if I could grab a stack of ballots and stuff the box for Grant. Maybe I could sniff some of that bonus. If there was a bonus, I corrected. The thought was unworthy of me anyway.

"And FIRST UP, to whet your appetites…a newcomer to the squared circle here in Wilmington, Delaware. Fighting out of Point Pleasant, Ohio…U.S. GRANT…to be opposed by BLAKE. IRONS."

With that, the crowd subsided into a kind of dull background roar. Daphne exited, repeating the routine of stepping down out of the ring by climbing down her escort's body. She sauntered off back to the backstage area. It was a world-class saunter in tuxedo pants that walked the edge from 'tailored' to 'painted on.' Under usual circumstances I would've felt a little slimy for watching as closely as I did, but clearly the woman was a performer. I was admiring her skill and professionalism.

The arena's sound system suddenly blared out a bugle call. I wasn't sure which one, because the quality of the sound system, plus the crowd's reaction, made it a little hard to identify. Some long suppressed, nearly forgotten military instinct in me suddenly woke up, poised to jump into action. Had it been a boatswain's whistle I probably would've broken out into a cold sweat at the very least.

Grant came sauntering into the arena, arms raised high, cavalry hat jauntily cocked. The bugle call kept repeating. There was a bit of a buzz for him, but not as much as one might have expected. That was, until he snatched a Confederate flag someone had been dangling over the barrier and ran with it to the ring. He leapt up to the ringside and threw the flag to the mat.

A few boos rained down.

Then he swung between the ropes, caught the flag with the spur of one boot, pinned it to the mat with the other, and ripped it in half with a wide kick of his legs.

While the boos weren't really overriding the cheers, I think I was starting to get an idea of why Grant was facing threats in other cities on this circuit.

While he was tearing that flag to shreds, someone had crept up ringside and took Grant's hat, handing him a mic.

"WILMINGTON," he called out, shouting the word so loud and so heavily into the mic that he invited feedback, and the crowd did worse than boo—they went quiet.

He tried again, getting it a little more right this time.

"Wilmington!"

There was scattered applause. "I've got a very special guest here tonight!"

Oh no.

"A veteran!"

Oh shit.

"A veteran of THE. UNITED. STATES. NAVY."

Oh fuck.

He pointed to me at ringside. There was thunderous applause. I was blinded by a light being swung into my eyes. "Look at him, ladies and gentlemen! I don't have to tell you what he risked for your freedom!"

What did I risk? Sodium poisoning through contact with the food? Cutting myself with a dull knife? Scalding from a steamtable?

The applause wasn't going away. Neither was the spotlight. I awkwardly waved a hand from my seat, and Grant seemed to get the hint that I wasn't going to do anything more than that.

I was saved from any further attention when Blake Irons trotted out. I had no idea what Blake's real name was, but there was no gimmick to him in the way that there was for Grant. Not that I could see. He was wearing a black singlet, black boots, elbow pads, and had his wrists wrapped in black tape. He looked a little creaky, to be honest, with a beard that was clearly dyed dark brown, his head shaved. There was almost no applause for him, and his facial expression was completely indifferent. Sweat beaded his head and his back, whether from the lights or anticipation or if he'd been warming up backstage, I couldn't say.

There was a scattered effort to start a chant of his first name, "Blake! Blake! Blake!" rung out weakly around the crowd, but it died out quickly after he acknowledged it with a wave.

In the interim, a ref had appeared. Blake and Grant moved to the center of the ring and shook hands. If any specific instructions were issued I didn't see them. Then the two men bounded off to opposite corners while the ref raised his arm in the middle of the ring. Then he lowered it.

I wasn't sure what I expected. Certainly not anything resembling the collegiate or Olympic sports I recognized. An immediate flurry of highly stylized, carefully faked violence? Someone to immediately leap in the air and deliver a flying kick?

They both fell into something resembling the neutral position, though both too upright. Blake especially so. I had the sense there wasn't a lot of flexibility left in him. He made a sloppy forward lunge and swung a big looping fist awkwardly at Grant.

Grant caught it and twisted Blake's arm, forcing his opponent to his knees. That move, at least, seemed pretty convincing as far as the crowd was concerned. Blake's face was twisted in pain and he sank to his knees. Grant moved up behind him and took hold of the back of his neck with the hand that wasn't twisting the arm. Blake's free arm flailed uselessly, raining harmless blows on his opponent's arm and side.

Then—as if a hand light on the back of the neck is a sufficient come-along hold on a person who isn't otherwise restrained—Grant let go of the twisted arm and 'pulled' Blake to his feet. Then he tugged him backwards and sent him running at the ropes. Blake took a workmanlike run-up to them, leaned far out, and immediately ran back at Grant as if helpless before the momentum.

Grant met him with a clothesline and Blake threw himself hard to the mat, rebounding off the canvas with a great clatter. He definitely made me feel his fall; I had to give him that. Grant jumped on him for the pin but Blake kicked out of it before the ref could bring his arm down a third time, and immediately rolled to his side, then climbed back to his feet using the ropes. It was Grant's turn to go on the attack, and he did. They traded back and forth shots for a while, occasionally engaging in something that looked a little like real grappling. If you turned your head and squinted and couldn't see it really well, I suppose it would pass.

It was hard for me not to look at it that way, in light of a sport I'd spent almost a decade learning. It had probably been the thing I was best at, period. Not cooking, not investigating, not even sitting on my boat and drinking. I had started blowing away my high school competition as a tenth-grader, and started winning right away in college. Even though I hadn't wanted to answer Gen's dad earlier, if I'd really wanted it—been willing to sacrifice whatever else there was in my life for it—the Olympics weren't necessarily out of reach.

And yet to actually think of it again took watching athletes pretend—sort of—to wrestle.

I was jolted out of my self reflection and self pity by a roar from the crowd. They were engaged in another grapple with their heads grinding together. Suddenly, Grant squatted beneath Blake and lifted him into the air on his shoulders, straight up, Blake's legs twisting in the air. He held him there for a moment, the crowd actually invested in the match, rapt, and then jumped and brought Blake down to the mat beneath him. Blake lay, writhing in pain, and I wasn't sure how much was for the show. Grant covered him, the ref counted three, and his warm-up match was over.

The crowd seemed relatively entertained by the match's conclusion, and Grant got a pretty sustained cheer. Instead of celebrating the way I might have expected—going to the corners to raise them into a frenzy—he bent down and helped his opponent back to his feet. *That* got some applause. They shared a kind of handshake hug, the no-hard-feelings, good-game kind of thing I recognized from my sporting days. Then a ringside attendant tossed Grant his hat and he left, victorious, Blake trailing after him, limping.

I would not have been able to make an accurate guess at how much of that limp was real and how much was for show.

Chapter 11

Shortly thereafter, Daphne came back ringside, though without her sidemen, and took up the mic to announce the next match, though it was only moments before some music I vaguely recognized started playing over the loudspeakers, and a man in a suit and mirrored sunglasses came striding down the tunnel, a metal attaché case shackled to his wrist. If the poster was to be believed, this was Derrick Rigg.

Then I realized that the music was the theme from the old soap opera *Dallas*, and the pun that was his name, and I wasn't sure if I wanted to laugh or hold my head in my hands for not having gotten it sooner.

The crowd booed when Rigg tore the mic away from Daphne, but it was a lusty boo, an appreciative boo, a booing that said, yeah, you're evil and we're meant to boo you, but we love it.

"I understand," he boomed into the mic, in an exaggerated Texas drawl, "that there are some *ladies* here who think they can take on Derrick Rigg in the ring. Now, now…as a gentleman, I do not believe it is *right* to inflict any violence upon the fairer sex."

Daphne put on such a sneer as he said the fairer sex that the crowd erupted in cheers for her.

"But if I am challenged, I must also reply in order to uphold that very honor."

I decided that Derrick Rigg sounded like what'd you'd get if J.R. Ewing and Foghorn Leghorn had a son.

"So if you've got…"

With that, the loudspeakers blared again. "Are they playing *My Country Tis of Thee?*" I wondered aloud.

The guy in the seat next to me, who'd been tapping away at a phone the size of a tablet throughout the entire match—and had shown no sign of putting it away yet—absently said, "Nah, it's *God Save the Queen*. Spitfire's entrance music."

"Huh."

Derrick Rigg looked as dazed as if it was the first time he'd ever heard recorded music mechanically reproduced, and then a tall redhead in a British-flag-print leotard and tall red Doc Martens came running down the tunnel.

I was suddenly interested. The guy with the giant phone took some interest in me then.

"So is that true? You a veteran?"

"Huh? Yeah," I said. "But I didn't sacrifice anything. I was a cook."

He nodded and made some notes.

"What are you taking notes for?" I looked down at him, trying to see the screen of his phone, but he hunched his shoulders.

"I write for Squaring the Circle," he said, as if I should know what that meant. I stared at him till he turned to face me.

He was probably my age, with round glasses, soft cheeks, a light dusting of stubble over his pale skin.

"And that is?" I finally said.

"A wrestling blog?" He sounded a bit indignant that he'd had to explain.

"Ah. I don't really follow, the, uh…scene."

"How'd you get these seats then?"

"Old friend of Grant's."

That got his attention. "U.S. Grant's?"

"Well, uh, I just knew him as Grant."

He stuck a hand out. "Tommy Wilkerson," he said.

"Jack Dixon." I took his hand. It was a little sweaty, but this close to the lights, so was mine. His grip had more wiry strength in it than I would've guessed.

"That dedicating his match to a vet thing is all part of Grant's gimmick," he said. "Does it at every match. I sometimes wonder if the person he singles out is even a vet."

"Gimmick?"

"Yeah, you know, his character, his schtick, his angle."

Meanwhile, in the ring, Spitfire was shouting in Derrick Rigg's face, incoherently, while he looked on, amused, free hand in his pocket.

Daphne was trying to separate them, to no avail.

"They been teasing the build up between these two for so long I'm beginning to think they're never gonna book the match," Tommy said. "And they'd better hurry, because either one of these two is likely to get poached any day now."

"Hrm?"

"They're too good for DWF," he said. "Rigg's too solid a character, and Spitfire is, well..." He gestured at her. The heels on her Docs put her well over six feet tall, and she was in shape. Certainly she was worth gesturing at. "She's fearless," he said. "She'll climb anything, fly off of anything, bleed the hard way..."

"Bleed?"

He nodded. "They'll do weapons matches if they think the crowd will go for it." He looked around the building and said, "Probably too much of a suburban crowd here. Too many kids. But she'll take a bat right to the abs."

"Jesus."

He shrugged. "Sometimes it's what people want."

Meanwhile, Rigg had just finished proclaiming that he just didn't see one woman as a challenge. Spitfire grabbed the mic and said, "Well, you're in luck then, yank." She pointed to the tunnel and more music started. I recognized it, vaguely, but I could only have told you it was associated with Russia in movies.

Out came a shape in a dark cloak, hood pulled up, with what seemed like a pair of green eyes glowing underneath of it.

"Huh," Tommy said. "Two-on-one?"

"Who's that?"

"The Night Witch," he said. "Been both an enemy and an ally of Spitfire but it looks like they're teasing a team-up here."

"That has…interesting historical connotations," I said.

"Huh?"

"Spitfires were British WWII aircraft. The Night Witches were a unit of female Russian bomber pilots…"

"Well, I guess that makes sense," Tommy said. "Can I use that?"

"Sure," I said.

Night Witch was making a slow and stately progress toward the ring. Rigg was backing away, having ripped his aviators off, eyes wide and wild, as if in fear. Spitfire was glaring at him with a sweet and dangerous smile on her face.

God help me, I was getting interested.

And it was just then that my old pal Glen tapped me on the shoulder.

"Grant's ready to talk to you backstage," he whispered.

Chapter 12

I had followed Glen reluctantly. A part of me was surprised at how effective the show had been at capturing my interest. I was disappointed to have to stop watching.

But work called.

I followed him once more into the backstage warren, this time he led me to a different dressing room. There were some snacks laid out here, but more selectively—sports drinks, protein bars, packets of gel, fruit, cheese that didn't look like it had been sitting under a light for a week.

Grant, wearing a t-shirt and toweling at his sweaty head, was sitting on a folding chair. Blake Irons was there too, stretched out on the floor, his knees and elbows wrapped up in bandages with icepacks. His wrists, too, sat on the ground with icepacks above and beneath them.

I had to step carefully around him, and he said, "Sorry, gotta do the poor man's whirlpool, ain't got one in the clubhouse." I laughed a little and went to meet Grant, who was once again shaking my hand.

"What'd you think?"

"Ah, it was…well I'm not sure I'm equipped to judge, you know, but…it was good. I got invested. Ending was good."

"I'm thinking of calling that The Vicksburg," Grant said, with a grin. "You like it?"

"Uh, sure."

From the floor, Blake said, "You're gonna call it the career-ending herniated disc you don't learn to balance the weight better, kid." His voice told the story of a lifetime of sore joints and muscle spasms. I winced hearing it.

"I'm working on it, man, I'm working on it. Thank God I got you to help me sell it. So, Jack, you ready to come work for me?"

"Grant, I don't even know what you want me to do."

"I told you there's threats."

"Yeah, but that's not a particularly informative statement. Threats are also something you can take to the police."

"Yeah," he said, his face falling a little. "I, uh, would rather not go to the cops."

"I think this is my cue to get scarce," Blake said. Slowly, and so very obviously painfully that I was torn between offering help and being afraid that would be a blow to his dignity, Blake picked himself up. He bent down to try and collect his icepacks, pausing halfway down.

I stood, snatched them up, and handed them to him. He had to put a hand on his back to straighten himself up. He looked at me then when he did. His eyes were blue, his face wrinkled in pain.

"Thanks." He studied me for a second. "You were a wrestler, weren't you? I don't mean like this, I mean…"

"Yeah," Grant answered for me. "Damn good one too. Could've won us a National Championship…"

I waved the words away. "Long time ago," I said.

Blake nodded, perhaps sensing that I didn't much want to talk about it, then shuffled off. I think a shuffle was about as fast as he could move at that moment. Ice rustled and settled in the bags wrapped around his joints. He looked like some kind of golem made of ACE bandage and athletic tape and animated by pain rather than speech.

When we were finally alone, I turned on Grant.

"What the hell was that about, pointing me out at ringside?"

"I always try to point out a veteran as a tribute…"

"Yeah, well, don't make me one of 'em. I was just a cook, alright? Now why do you think you want to hire me?"

"I told you there've been threats against me."

"When? Where? What kind?"

"A phone call to a venue just after we left that said we should never come back. Couple emails. A letter."

"And what did the threats say?"

"That they'd kill me if I ever came back."

I grabbed a folding chair and pulled it to within a few feet of Grant. From the inside pocket of my jacket, I pulled out the firm's client-intake paperwork.

"This is cop stuff, Grant. Somebody makes a threat on your life, you call the police, and they determine whether it's credible. I'm the guy you call if you suspect a business partner is trying to screw you. Or your wife, I guess."

"Well…the company ain't real keen on calling the cops."

I resisted the urge to lift a hand to cover my eyes. I kept one hand on the paperwork and the other in a light fist on my lap. It was difficult.

"Why?"

He shrugged. "They don't want that kind of attention."

"Why?"

He sighed. "You know…lotta people work for the company. I mean, it's small, as promotions go. But beyond the talent, and the creative folks, you got the security, and the lighting and sound people, and the roadies…"

"And either there are enough illegal substances floating around, or enough folks with records—or on probation, or on parole, or who aren't supposed to be leaving a state—that nobody wants any actual police around."

"Pretty much," Grant confirmed.

"What do your own security people say?"

"That it's probably nothing to worry about."

"And why don't you trust that assessment?"

"Because they're basically just bouncers. Doormen. They aren't, you know…" He waved a hand vaguely in the air. "Investigators."

"Okay. Would it be you hiring me, or the company?"

"What do you cost?"

"Depends if we're talking retainer, how many hours…" I held out the paperwork and he scanned it quickly. His eyes suddenly widened.

"Uh, I think the company's gonna have to cover this."

I started wondering just how much Grant was making for risking his health and spine for the Delmarva Wresting Federation. But it was a rude question to ask this early.

"Well, then you better get the okay from somebody and get that paperwork filled out, and let me know when you want to start working."

He looked up. "Well, we've got the next week off. Thanksgiving, you know? But the Monday after that we go back on the road. Dover, couple of beach towns, down into Virginia, then around D.C., then up into PA…lotta wrestling fans in PA, ya know…"

"Wait. What exactly are you saying? You want me to travel with you?"

Grant smiled broadly. "Hell yeah, bro! On the bus, twenty-four hours a day, man."

"Provided the company can pay for it."

"They'll pay for it or I'll call the cops," he said, with a shrug. "Should be easy."

I thought that Grant's negotiating position wasn't as strong as he thought. It was likely that he was an independent contractor and had next to no recourse if he was fired. But I didn't have the heart or patience to try and explain that to him just then.

"You know I'm not a cop, so I can't arrest anyone or pull in cop resources. I'm also not really a bodyguard."

"You got this, man. I'm sure you do."

I sighed. "Alright. But if you want me on the bus, twenty-four hours a day…this isn't gonna be cheap."

"I'll call the boss right now," he said, waving the papers in his hand. "And we'll get you on the bus in Dover next Monday, okay?"

I still doubted his ability to get me hired in precisely the way he wanted. "I think your boss is gonna want to talk to me and, you know, understand what she'd be spending money on."

"Look, man, just show up in Dover next Monday. We'll get you on the bus, I guarantee it."

"Grant, I can't get on the bus unless I'm hired. Officially. Through the firm. That's the only way, legally speaking, for me to work for you or the company and be protected."

"What do you mean?"

"I mean…a lot of complicated legal stuff that I don't really understand, except that I'm under strict orders from my boss not to do any work unless I've got it all squared away."

"Alright. Cool. I'll text you the address. See you next Monday?"

"Sure," I said, without much feeling.

Chapter 13

I found an empty room and took the time to file some preliminary reports and what billing info I had via the firm's app on my phone. I wasn't really thrilled about the idea of going out on tour with the DWF.

But after doing some figuring of how many billable hours this would run up, I didn't see how I could turn it down. I also typed up an email to Jason, explaining the situation as I saw it. I included a note that I thought it unlikely they'd actually want to hire me in the way the principal—Grant—really wanted.

That done, I got back to my seat just in time to see Spitfire climbing a ladder that had been erected ringside. Meanwhile, the Night Witch was holding Derrick Rigg prone in the center of the ring in a leglock that would've dislocated his knee by now if it was being applied with malicious intent. He writhed and pounded the middle of the ring, appealing to the ref, who stood against the corner ropes in some kind of daze, totally unresponsive.

The crowd was in a frenzy, cheering, screaming, applauding, while Spitfire got to the top of the ladder and raised her arms to egg them on.

She spread her arms, bent her knees, and dove from the top of the ladder.

I found myself holding my breath.

She landed square atop Rigg with a tremendous, canvas rattling crash. Night Witch had rolled away and slipped out of the ring. The ref came out of his daze just in time to slap his hand on the mat three times and give the victory to the high-flying Englishwoman.

If the ending was anything to go by, I had to admit I kind of wished I'd seen the entire match. There was some post-match mic work, Daphne coming back out to work up the crowd, but it looked like the actual wrestling was over. I decided to head back out to the front and wait for Gen and her dad.

The crowd straggled out bit by bit while I leaned against the wall, between the wide open doors. Eventually the trickle became a flood, I spotted Gen the instant she came into view, and I glided up behind them, tapping her on the shoulder. We hit up a Mexican place for dinner while her dad gushed about some of the performances—particularly Spitfire's.

Thankfully neither of them asked about that little 'tribute' Grant had made. Perhaps they hadn't seen it. Regardless I spent the whole meal dreading answering any questions about it. And avoiding the chips.

Your standard Mexican restaurant menu didn't offer a lot of options that my typical diet would accommodate. I contemplated a selection of salads, eyed the enchiladas with lust in my heart, and settled on some fish tacos—after making sure the fish itself wasn't breaded.

They weren't bad, and I was happy to keep the conversation light. I was distracted—and not, as usual, by Gen. Or at least, not as much as usual. I was thinking about working, thinking about living on a bus and the road with a bunch of professional wrestlers and roadies for… how long? A couple of days? A week? A month?

I was pulled back to the reality of dinner by Gen asking me a question for a second time, then repeating my name. "Jack?"

"Ah, sorry," I muttered. "Just losing myself in thinking about this job Grant wants to hire me for."

"Which is what, exactly?"

"Eh, I'm not sure I can say. I don't even know if I've been hired yet. Something about threats."

I explained the offer I thought I had, to go on the road with them starting the following Monday.

"Sounds like good money," her dad said.

"How long will you be gone?"

"I think it would be, and I don't know."

Gen frowned for a moment, then steered the conversation back to the wrestling we'd watched. Bill seemed particularly impressed with Spitfire, lauding her leap from the ladder and speaking approvingly of how Rigg had sold the ending.

"Sold?"

He shrugged. "I mean, it's not like that leg lock the Witch had him in was all that restrictive, right? But he made it look good."

"What was going on with the ref?"

"That's the Witch's gimmick," Gen answered. "Temporarily stuns the ref with some kind of puff of smoke and light. Flash paper up her sleeve, probably. Never the opponent, because that'd be too easy, right?"

My days of watching wrestling were long past, and I hadn't really been that sophisticated a viewer. Seemed like I had a lot to learn.

Thankfully, I could be a quick study.

* * *

That night, back in Gen's apartment—with a backpack full of clothes and a dopp kit I'd picked up back at the *Belle*—it seemed like time to Talk. I wasn't thrilled about it. It had been so long since I'd had to Talk I wasn't sure I still knew how to do it.

"So," I began, as she leaned against me on the couch, some music playing softly from a streaming station on her TV.

"Yes?" She looked up at me from under her eyelashes and I almost forgot how to talk at all.

"I might be gone a while," I said. "I don't know how long…"

"Doesn't seem like you can really pass on it."

"Provided the company meets the firm's rates and covers expenses… yeah, I think I have to do it."

She sat up and put her back against one arm of her couch, looking at me directly. "And?"

"I just, uh. Where does that leave us?"

"Where are we starting from?"

"Right. That." I swallowed hard and looked at her. She was a beautiful woman, and a damn sight smarter than I'd assumed when we'd met in an office, the first morning of a new case, just a couple of months ago.

What was she even doing, sitting on a couch with me? Looking at me?

"I met your dad tonight."

"Yep," she said. "He likes you. Of course, taking him to his first wrestling show in years didn't hurt. He's not thrilled about the motorcycle, though." She smiled.

"So meeting your dad is kind of…a thing. Right? Isn't it?"

"What're you getting at, Jack?"

"Well, I guess…what's the term or the word for…you know, whatever we're…what am I?"

"Hrm." Gen's face got serious, her brow furrowed. "I think the conventional term is 'boyfriend.' Is that what you're asking?"

"Uh, it was, yeah. What I was asking."

She leaned forward. "And what do you think of the answer?"

"It's a good one. Pretty much the one I was hoping to hear."

"Good." She leaned forward further, till she was no longer sitting so much as kneeling across from me on the couch. She planted her hands on my shoulders and pushed me back. It took me by surprise and I fell back.

She climbed on top of me. I stopped asking questions.

Chapter 14

I opened the door into Jason's office, only to walk straight into his outthrust hand, one finger held up in the universal sign for 'silence.'

Like a cartoon character trying to be quiet, I took exaggerated steps from the door over to the French press. With dramatic care for the noise I made I lifted the press and selected a mug.

"I'm afraid our rates are non-negotiable," he was saying. His phone buzzed as the other person on the line spoke.

"I respect your position, Mr. Gogarty," he said. "But I can't budge on that."

More buzzing I couldn't hear. He looked at me, speculatively.

"I think that idea has some potential." He nodded, holding the phone to his ear with his shoulder, reaching for the pad of paper on his desk, and taking up a pen. He began writing with quick strokes, the pen audibly scratching against the paper. "Yeah. That sounds good. Sure, we've got a fax. He can start inquiries as soon as you make that deposit. Yeah, today, absolutely. Dent-Clark looks forward to working on your behalf." He hung up.

"Well," he said, "looks like you've got another job."

I poured my coffee. "I'm not a bodyguard."

"No, but for a gig that could last weeks or months like this one, you can figure out how to fake it."

"Meaning what?" I added my preferred yellow packets and dollop of dairy, probably half-and-half rather than the whole milk I would've preferred.

"Meaning once we get you kitted out, no one'll be able to tell you aren't the god damned Secret Service."

I took a sip of the coffee and tried not to roll my eyes. He always had the good stuff, at least.

"Does this mean I have to…"

"Yes, you're carrying a company piece while you're on this job. *And* we're getting you a vest."

"I've got a vest. A couple, actually. One fleece, one down…Eddie Bauer. It's great. Keeps me warm but leaves my arms free to whip hell out of bad guys."

He eyed me over his glasses.

"Nobody is gonna shoot at me at a wrestling show, man."

"Better to wear the vest and not need it than…"

I couldn't see a percentage in arguing. I took a seat.

"You don't really want this, do you? Do I need to put Brock on it?"

"We already know that getting shot doesn't bother him," I said. I regretted the words even before Jason's face darkened. "I'm sorry," I said, raising a hand immediately. "I'm sorry. I'm an asshole."

"Yeah, but you're my asshole. And besides, we both know this is a bona fide mystery—and you won't be able to let go of it before you figure it out."

"Don't even know what 'it' is yet," I said. "Haven't seen any of the threats or been filled in."

"Company owner…that's Oscar Gogarty, who I was on the phone with…is going to send over everything they've got so far."

"What was the negotiating about?"

"He was looking for ways to lower the rates."

"And what'd you settle on?"

"Regular hourly rates with enough retainer for two weeks," Jason said. "But no expenses."

"No expenses? How the hell do I make any money on the job then?"

He held up that 'silence' finger again. "You're gonna be traveling with the company, staying in hotels with the company, eating with the company…his point was that they'd be floating all your expenses anyway, so there was no need for it."

"That's fair, I guess…but what do I do about food? Eat at craft services every night?"

"They'll give you the same per diem they give employees."

"What kind of employees? Crew? Creative? Talent?"

"I did not ask. Besides, how much does a jar of peanut butter cost you?"

"Some of the peanut butter I eat? More than you'd expect." I finished the coffee with my usual gulp, since it hadn't really been hot to begin with. "I don't know what to make of this thing at all. Seems like Grant just has a character that pisses some of the crowd off and somebody wrote a dumb letter."

"And you will be diligent in tracking down said dumb letter writer and exposing their nefarious plot for all the world to see. And as it might take a few weeks, you've got the chance to make some real money."

"My lifestyle is cheap."

"How's your girlfriend like the boat?"

A couple of protests surged up. First about the word girlfriend, but that had been pretty thoroughly settled just a couple of nights ago. The other was to ask what that had to do with anything, but then I realized the implication.

"I'm not moving to dry land. Not to any of the dry land I can afford, anyway."

"You're nothing if not committed to the aesthetic. Go on out and grab a desk and start a file. I'll give you whatever they send over."

* * *

I had the case file open and the various principals and locations cross referenced before I heard anything from Delmarva Wrestling. Jason CC'd me an email that had a PDF. Once I got it open, it looked like a PDF scan made with somebody's phone of a fairly wrinkled piece of paper.

In irregular but legible cursive, the letter read:

The South is a proud place and Our Heritage will not be subjected to the insults of your company's U.S. Grant. He had better never perform in Virginia again. Not in Norfolk or Virginia Beach. Not in Richmond or Bristol nor anywhere in between or there will be serious consequences.

It was signed *The Knights of the South.* There was some kind of mark on the paper next to that name, but the paper had been so wrinkled and the scan so bad I couldn't really make out what it was.

"Oh, boy," I muttered. I spent a couple of minutes lamenting the state of history education in the country over the past several decades that had allowed anyone to believe specious bullshit about the south's 'heritage' in regards to the Civil War, and all its symbols.

Frankly, my sympathy was entirely with the guy tearing up the rebel flag.

I did some searching for The Knights of the South. The hits were so many and varied that I decided to try narrowing it via some official lists of hate groups published by various watchdogs. Nothing there. I narrowed my searches and spent the next hour wading through some of the worst web design and dumbest ideas I'd ever seen.

There were plenty of groups that had similar names or similar motifs—lots of Crusader Crosses, or imitation Crusader Crosses. Lots of Celtic crosses with bad spiral knot-work in the circles. But nothing that jumped out at me; no exact match for The Knights of the

South associated with any of the locations named in the letter, or even Virginia in general. The letter was not getting me anywhere.

By the time I'd looked into all that, I had several more emails. The first one I opened was a massive wall of text of different fonts. For a moment I was put in mind of the classic movie ransom letter where all the words are cut out of different sources.

Then I realized what I was looking at was a series of comments cut and pasted from various wrestling message boards, press releases, and articles about Delmarva Wrestling and U.S. Grant in particular.

I read a few of them.

So stiff in the ring…

Seems like a real asshole…

His gimmick is gonna get him killed if they ever go to the Deep South…

Going to hurt someone with that finisher…

I stopped about halfway down the first page. I wrote a quick email to Jason.

"I'll do a lot of things for this job. But I'm not going to spend hours reading the damn comments."

I paged through the rest of what they sent me. A poor recollection of a threatening call they'd gotten at a show in southern Maryland. No details to work with, just the hourly worker who'd picked up the phone at company HQ recalling someone had said they didn't want to see Grant performing that character again, and that there'd be trouble if he did.

I made a note on the file: *ask for audio.* No way of knowing if they had it, but it couldn't hurt to ask.

That was it. That was all I had to go on. I summarized my findings in an email to my boss and thought about the upcoming week, and my least favorite holiday.

For me, Thanksgiving was beneath Earth Day, Arbor Day, Flag Day, and goddamned Garbage Ape Day if they ever declared one.

The following Saturday, now that was a day I cared about. That was a day I could spend with people I enjoyed seeing. And lately things had been going too well, and I'd been in too good a mood to deal with it.

I made the executive decision to skip it entirely, and I passed the next day ignoring any and call phone calls. Since none were from Gen, Dani, or Jason, I spent the entire day cleaning the boat, making sure it was winterized, and thinking about Saturday.

For my own personal Thanksgiving dinner, I had a third of a bottle of Wigle bourbon and about half a jar of Wild Friends Pumpkin Spice Peanut Butter, which seemed the most seasonally appropriate thing in my cupboard.

Chapter 15

I should have spent Friday morning making a brine of vegetable broth, ginger, salt, brown sugar, pepper, and allspice at Dani's house. I should've been helping Emily roll out baguette loaves.

Instead, I had been called into the office just after nine a.m.

It was a cold day, the promise of winter in it. We didn't get much of a fall in these parts anymore; typically it stayed warm through October, then it seemed as though all the trees shed their leaves all at once, in the first week of November, and now it was all just a boring prelude to winter.

When I got there I saw Jason's car in the lot, as well as what I thought was the Lexus driven by Mrs. Jackson's attorney.

My heart sank into my stomach, where it bubbled menacingly with the bourbon I'd had for Thanksgiving dinner.

Nobody else was in the office, and I thought I heard raised voices in Jason's office. So I made my way there and shoved right in without waiting for an invite.

"Jack," Jason said. He was dressed casually, a polo shirt over jeans, which I almost never saw him in. But then, it was the Friday after Thanksgiving. Nobody worked then; not even him.

I nodded. "Ms. Hanes." The attorney was wearing a loose gray sweater over dark blue jeans that looked expensive, and heeled boots. It was casual-as-dressy.

"Just what do you think you were doing, assaulting my client's husband. Do you realize how this complicates her case? I'm here to get back every damn dime she paid you."

"Assaulting your client's husband?"

"Yes, and he said there'd be witnesses. Said you even tried to steal his car."

I walked over to the conference table and set down my helmet and gloves.

"Ms. Hanes. If I had truly wanted to steal Donald Jackson's car, would he have been able to stop me?"

"He says he threatened to call the police."

I sighed. "Ms. Hanes, where does he say this occurred?"

"At a gas station a few blocks away from the firm."

"How does he know where the firm is?"

"It's public knowledge."

"Right." Behind her I saw Jason starting to grin. "And did he use my name or describe me?"

"He referred to you as Jack."

"So your suggestion here is that I was stupid enough to brace Mr. Jackson and *give him my name*."

"He says a bystander called you that."

"Huh. Ms. Hanes, did it occur to you to ask Mrs. Jackson how her soon to be ex-husband knew who had handled the investigation into his infidelity? Not the firm, I mean, but the individual."

"No, I just got a phone call from his attorney and…"

"Immediately sped over here on Black Damn Friday, America's favorite holiday, to try and get money back?"

"It's my job to defend the interests of my client."

"Your client told her husband who I was. She told him I rode a bike, and what kind, and what I looked like, and where to find me."

"How do you know that?" She was put off. I don't think she'd expected me to be anything but surprised.

"Because a few days ago he tried to run me off the road. Then he followed me to the firm and attacked me."

"Well," I could see gears clicking behind her lawyer's eyes. I liked her a little less, though I understood where it came from. Best interests of her client indeed. "That would change things. How did you respond?"

"I defended myself." I saw her eyes start to widen, and I raised a hand. "*Gently*," I said. "I didn't hurt him. I did take away his keys for a little while, because he was clearly at the end of a three-martini lunch, and I didn't want to put him back on the road. I told him to walk to the gas station and back for coffee and to cool off. Eventually I gave him his keys back. And your client sent him after me because she wanted him at least humiliated, probably roughed up."

"Are you willing to appear in court in order to…"

"No," I said flatly. "Not unless Mr. Jackson tries to press charges."

"But this could mean…"

"I don't care," I said, cutting her off, rudely, which I immediately felt badly about. But I had the initiative and I soldiered on. "Look, my work for Mrs. Jackson is finished. I don't want to go back on the clock for it, and frankly, I'm out of town for a long time starting Monday. I don't blame you for looking out for Mrs. Jackson, and that's all you thought you were doing. But we've wasted enough time on this."

Ms. Hanes reached into the small purse she carried. It had an expensive looking designer's marque on it, but I could never tell one of those apart from another. She handed me a card.

"You may hear from me," was all she said before walking out. We both watched her leave, waited to hear the door close.

Looking at the card, seeing her name in black and white, it finally occurred to me to ask.

"Ms. Hanes," I said, and she paused at the door of Jason's office. "How's Liza?"

She lifted an eyebrow as a question. She had pinpoint control of her features; I don't know if that was a lawyer thing, but I bet it helped.

"Did she never mention me? I found her friend Gabriel after he dropped out of school."

The eyebrow lift that was a question melted into widened eyes of comprehension. "Of course she did. She never gave me your last name, but...I probably should've made the connection on my own."

I shrugged. "Not like it occurred to me either."

"My daughter did seem to think well of you, which is unusual for her and...any adult."

I chuckled. "We all go through that phase, but...she seemed like a good kid. The kind who worried about her friends. If you doubt the account I've just given you, maybe ask her if she thinks I'm a liar."

"I will," she said, and I was convinced she was going to go do just that as she shut the door and walked out.

"I've never known anyone who could impress someone *while* pissing them off quite like you, Jack," Jason said, with a little laugh.

"We all have our gifts." I turned to Jason. "How good can she be if she fell for that bullshit from the Jackson asshole?"

He shrugged. "Took her off guard, I guess. And this is a divorce attorney's busy season anyway."

"November?"

"The holidays. Nothing to make you realize you hate your family like being forced to spend time with 'em."

"Hell," I said, feeling a little sick, "I don't need to spend any time with my family to know that."

The lighter tone vanished. Jason cleared his throat and said, "Well, the DWF still wants you Monday. Let's get you kitted out. I'm going of town this weekend."

He reached into his pocket for keys.

I knew better than to argue the point. If this was a bodyguarding job, I knew I needed to carry something, even if I didn't much like it.

First, he set down a Taser, yellow and blue in a plastic belt holster. Then a box of 9mm ammo. A small black plastic case, locked. A couple key-ring sized pepper spray dispersal units.

He turned to me. "You want a shoulder rig or a belt?"

"Uh, shoulder I guess. Be able to wear it under a jacket then."

A leather strap with two loops for shoulders hit his desk. Then, finally, a vest.

"Really? A vest?"

"If people are serious about attacking you'll be glad you have it."

"I've already got Kevlar in my jacket."

"It won't look suspicious at all if you follow him around wearing a motorcycle jacket zipped to the chin all the damn time."

"Fine, fine."

He used a smaller key to open the black plastic case. Inside it was a Beretta Storm 9mm.

"We could probably do the subcompact if you really wanna go concealed…"

"Doesn't matter," I said. "Let's just get this over with."

"You're gonna wear it now."

"I'm here on the bike, and I don't have saddlebags to get any of this home. Plus I don't have a safer place to leave it between now and Monday."

"Well, don't sleep with it on."

"Don't plan to." I took my jacket off and Jason looped the rig over my arms. There were pockets for two magazines under my right arm and the holster under my left. He held out the case and I reluctantly took the gun. There was one spare magazine. I ejected the one in the pistol, checked the slide to be sure it was unloaded, then slid it into the holster.

Goddamn but I hated wearing a weapon. I'd hated it in the Marine Police and I hated it now. Reluctantly, I slid the jacket back over it, then said, "There a spare gym bag or something around for the rest of this?"

"Go look for something," Jason said.

I hunted through the various cubicles; eventually I found a large reusable shopping bag. I was going to feel damn strange carrying it on my bike back to the *Belle* but there we were.

When I came into his office with it, my boss looked like he was reconsidering. "You're going to put a Taser and a block of ammo and a vest into a shopping bag and, what? Stick it in your chain locker?"

"No. I'm going to leave the vest and the pepper spray in a locker on my boat. I think I know a more secure place for the rest of it."

"Fine. Don't you dare lose my firearm."

"I can't lose it if you don't make me take it with me."

"Not arguing about this. Now go do some shopping or whatever it is you do on days off."

I knew I was up against one of his limits, so off I went. After storing the vest and the pepper spray on the *Belle* I texted Dani.

You still got a locker in the garden shed?

Yeah. Why?

I'm on my way but I've got a package.

Fine.

Chapter 16

Without Emily seeing it or knowing about it, I met Dani around the back of their house and, true to her word, she had a fairly secure looking locker in the garden shed and woodshop behind their house. The locker was sort of half-hidden behind some stacks of plans and odds and ends of wood.

"You don't worry about this locker being outside the house," I asked, suddenly wondering at it.

"The base is attached to the concrete pad under the shed," Dani replied. "To move it you'd need a jackhammer or dynamite. Either way I assume I'd notice."

"Fair."

I turned while she spun the lock open. Then, and only then, did I unzip my jacket.

"You really got to come to my house armed?"

"Boss didn't give me a choice," I said. "Apparently for this job, I'm going armed whether I want to or not."

From the shopping bag I took out the gun case Jason had given me. I slipped the pistol out of my shoulder rig and locked it in the case, then handed it over.

There were a couple weapons in the locker: a shotgun and a pistol, it looked like. Boxy-looking Glock, probably something in the .40

range. I wasn't too interested and Dani wasn't going to offer details on her own. I also handed her the box of ammo and pulled the Taser off my belt.

"Jesus, Jack. What is it you're doing next?"

"Protecting a professional wrestler from angry fans. I think."

"Nothing about that sentence made it any clearer."

"You ain't the only one who's confused."

"Well, if it's that dangerous, you want to borrow a baton or something?"

"Honestly, I'd rather carry one of those than a gun any day. That a serious offer?"

"Yeah." Dani reached into the safe and pulled out two sheathed cylindrical objects. Telescoping batons.

"Are these things even legal in all the surrounding states?"

"It varies. You've got licenses, right? That might give you some cover. And besides, if it comes down to it, do you really give a shit if the weapon in your hand is legal or not?"

"I suppose I don't." I took the one she held out to me. It had a tactical rubber grip on the end and was tightly fitted into a nylon sheath with a belt loop. "Better leave it in the safe for now. But thanks. I'll take it tomorrow."

Off we went for more work. Emily had made good progress in my absence but I still had to work at a quick pace to try and catch up. I spent about an hour doing nothing but chopping onions, mushrooms, apples, and then peeling hot chestnuts for the more traditional dressing we'd serve tomorrow. The other, a corn bread pudding, was quick and mercifully easy, with almost no prep work. All we'd need to do was leave out one of the baking loaves to get a little hard and stale overnight.

When I came up for air, wiping sweat off my forehead with my sleeve, Emily handed me a cold pint glass. I sniffed it carefully and it smelled delicious; spicy, a little sweet, rich.

"Southern Tier Pumking," she said. "Best part of the season."

"I find that point hard to argue with," I said. I still peered at it a little mistrustfully. "Any idea what the ABV is?"

"Jack, if you're worried about riding home, you know you can always just stay here. If you're worried about the calories," she said, dropping her voice. "You shouldn't be."

I took a deep breath and then a tiny sip of the beer. It was so good I wanted to tip it back and finish it in one go. Instead I stuck with the cautious sip.

"That," I said, "is delicious. Thank you." I set the mug down but gave it a longing look as I did, and went back to chopping and assembling.

"Dani tells me you're bringing a young lady tomorrow," Emily said, as she checked the loaves she had in the oven.

"I am."

"This is a first."

"Yup."

"Are you going to tell me anything about her?"

I laughed. "It's…hard to find the right words, I guess. I have a hard time talking about her. Or even…to her."

"How'd you meet? Let's start there."

"Uh, on my last case, actually. The missing kid, Gabriel? Gen… Geneva…works for his father. I spoke to her early in the investigation. Later she…well, she gave me the info that broke the case for me."

"Is there anything unethical about dating someone you meet that way?"

"Well, we didn't actually start dating till after the case had concluded."

"That sounds like a technicality, Jack."

"Maybe it is, but I took her to dinner to thank her for her help and…here we are."

She nodded. We went silent again. "You haven't been in the woodshop lately You're good with tools. You enjoy working with your hands and it's probably good for your soul."

"I know…I just…"

"Well. Might be a good time to think about making something. Maybe a Christmas present for your Geneva?"

"That's…not a bad idea at all."

We went back to work; we sipped beer, chopped, cooked, assembled, baked, and my head spun with the idea Emily had planted in it.

Chapter 17

I was outside in the parking lot of the marina bright and early Saturday morning.

Well, it was early, anyway. Late November wasn't any too bright at that time of day. Or any time of day, really. At least it wasn't raining. Yet.

Gen's car pulled up at the stroke of eight. With my knife roll and a bag of assorted other tools—I was particular about things like towels and oven mitts—I trotted up and slid into the passenger door as she unlocked it.

I looked across at her in the driver's side and my breath caught. She was wearing jeans that fit well—not in that constricting movement way I'd seen more often these days—boots without heels, a button up shirt with the collar pulled out atop a rust-red sweater, and a stylish light blue peacoat. Her hair was still wet from the shower, and slicked back, it emphasized her high cheekbones, her chin, the way she was smiling at me. She wore makeup, subtly done, but enough to emphasize her eyes and make their size seem like some kind of special effect.

"What?"

"You're...perfect. That's all."

"Flatterer," she said, putting a hand on my arm and leaning across the console to kiss my cheek.

"Well," I said, flushing a little at how mush-mouthed I got around her. "It's true. Wherever we go, whatever we do together, you always... just, look perfect for it."

She laughed as she put her car in gear. "You know, you usually look pretty good yourself."

"Usually?"

"I have only ever seen you in a suit the once, Jack. I could handle another view."

"I should've gone shopping yesterday."

She chuckled. "How was your Thanksgiving?"

"It was great. I sat on my boat and read all day."

She paused in the parking lot. "Your family situation is...that bad?"

I shrugged. "You're meeting the people who matter most today."

That seemed like a good answer. I pulled up the GPS on my phone. Gen had one of those suction-cup devices on her windshield, so I plugged it in there. "How was yours?"

"It was good. My dad asked about you. Said he was hoping I might bring you with me."

"If I had the choice to make over again," I said, trailing off intentionally.

She chuckled again and we drove in silence for a bit.

"So...how many people will be here?"

"At one time? Maybe twenty. I'll know five of them and...there's really only two I want you to meet."

"Danielle, and..."

"Her wife Emily.

"And they do..."

"Dani's a physician's assistant and sometime paramedic. Emily is a Unitarian minister."

"Unitarian?"

"I'm not real clear on the theology but she won't talk about it unless you ask. And even then, she's pretty uncanny about knowing how much someone actually wants to hear. She's no kind of fire and brimstone preacher."

"Good to know. What'll the menu be like?"

"For breakfast, there'll be fresh baked bread, honey-butter, coffee, tea, and fruit. Finger foods and cheeses in the late morning and early afternoon until dinner is served. It'll be the standard Thanksgiving menu but…"

"Better?"

"I didn't want to insult your family's cooking, but hopefully. I put the turkey in a brine yesterday and I'll pack it beneath the skin with compound butter before it roasts. Couple of ducks are hanging and will be ready to roast. There's three kinds of dressing, there'll be a roasted root vegetable casserole…"

"You doing all of this?"

"Sort of…overseeing it, I guess. Emily's a better baker than I am so most of the bread and such is on her."

"Can I ask a question?"

"Of course."

"If you can whip up this kind of spread for twenty people in two days, why *aren't* you cooking for a living?"

"Because it doesn't accommodate my workout schedule."

"Really, though. Why not?"

"It's hot and boring and repetitive and never-ending. It exploits the workers pretty thoroughly. If I went and applied at a chain restaurant around the mall, I'd get hired in a heartbeat. And because I'm a white guy and a veteran, I'd immediately get put in charge over immigrants who've been working their asses off in kitchens for twenty or thirty years."

"Didn't think about it that way."

"At the end of the day I'd have a lot more responsibility and not a whole lot more money."

"Wouldn't want to start your own restaurant?"

My stomach actually flipped menacingly at the words. "Oh, God, no," I said, practically groaning. "I could not handle that kind of stress."

We drove in silence for a little while. Finally I brought up the subject I didn't want to.

"You know I've…gotta go out of town on Monday. I don't know for how long."

"I know. And let's put that under things *I* don't want to talk about, okay?"

"Done," I said. I slid my hand near the console and she took one of hers off the steering wheel long enough to grab it and squeeze it. I tried to gather up the anticipation of Monday, of my absence, of whatever stupidity or danger I was likely to encounter, and shove it away from me. Live in the moment, I told myself. I had never been great at that.

I was bringing Geneva Lawton to meet my closest friends and spend one day of the damn year eating whatever I wanted. If I couldn't live in this moment, when could I?

Chapter 18

The morning was magnificent. Dani and Emily had all their windows open and the cold morning air streamed through a house that would soon be full of people and the heat of cooking. I went outside to build the coals that the ducks would roast over in their grill. While I was out there I poured the brine out of the cooler with the turkey in it into their compost.

When I carried the bird and cooler in, Gimli—their enormous orange cat—met me at the door, being suspiciously affectionate.

"Not for you, big guy."

The look he gave me, and the yawning display of his teeth, was meant to make me reconsider my haste and my error. It didn't work, so he trotted off in search of an easier con.

Gen, to her credit, immediately pitched in to help wherever she could. With her sweater off and her sleeves rolled up, an apron on, arms plunged into the sink to wash dishes we'd need again soon, she was no less beautiful than she'd been picking me up, or on our first date.

"You've got it bad," Dani murmured out of the side of her mouth, as she passed by me with a stack of small plates, having caught me staring at my own date.

"Yeah," I agreed. "You blame me?"

"Nope."

By the time I could sit down with a hunk of bread and a too-thick double spoonful of honey butter to swipe it across, Gen had found one of the photos on the wall and waved me over.

She pointed to it. "When was this?"

"Well, you may note from the formal attire that it was a wedding. Dani and Emily's, in point of fact."

"Are you wearing a kilt?"

"Yes."

"Do you still *have* it?"

"Rental."

"Ever think about getting one?"

"I am now."

"Good."

She briefly ducked her head against my shoulder while I chewed. I felt like eyes were on me and I turned and found Emily, in jeans and a sweatshirt and apron, grinning madly. I blushed, finished my breakfast, and got back to work.

Behind me, I heard Emily stage whisper something about kilts. I buried myself in work, flushing furiously but also feeling something curious and unexpected. I think it was happiness.

* * *

I don't know if I was lucky, but I got the ducks off the indirect roasting heat and the turkey out of the oven and resting within five minutes of one another. I always like working with coals and open flames but I never quite trust myself; this was probably the best work I'd ever done with it. Both ducks were covered in crisp skin, the best of all delicacies. I was carefully arranging oyster dressing around them both on a huge wooden platter when I felt a hand on my shoulder and then Gen's chin resting on my arm.

"Why not stuff them while they cook?"

I shook my head. "An invitation to cross-contaminating at best. Like building a hotel for food poisoning at worst."

"But the dressing gets those crunchy bits that way."

I turned around, smiling at her, and set down my spoon and bowl of stuffing. I went to the tool bag I'd brought and removed a culinary torch, adjusted the knobs, and lit it.

"You want crunchy dressing, you got it," I said. In truth I was very sparing with the torch—what I wanted out of my dressing was for it to be flavorful and filling and crunch wasn't a textural goal for me. But Gen was getting what she wanted if I was cooking.

By the time the turkey had been similarly prepared for presentation, a big crowd had gathered. I knew enough of them to not feel out of place—neighbors, friends, folks who'd been involved in Dani and Emily's wedding three and a half years ago—but being on cooking detail meant I didn't have to spend a lot of time making small talk. It looked like Gen was holding up the side in that regard, though. From the looks on the faces of people who talked to her—many asking who she was and how she knew Dani and Emily, from the number of times I saw her gesture towards me—everybody seemed to find her as charming as I did.

Of course they did. Who wouldn't?

With tables finally set and me and Dani having carved the various birds and the buffet lining up, Gen slid up next to me again. I put my arm around her and she did the same.

"Okay. What's good, and what's low carb?"

I looked down at her with my eyes wide and she laughed, took a plate from the stack, and avoided nothing.

I made room on my first plate only for duck, turkey, and stuffing—all three kinds. If I was going to eat carbs, by God I was going to eat carbs.

About halfway through that plate I snuck my phone out of my pocket and held it in my hand. I heard the sound of a throat cleared across the table from me. Emily, an eyebrow delicately arched.

Sheepishly, I tucked it back into my pocket.

I could count all the calories later.

As dinner progressed, Emily set her sights on Gen.

"Geneva," she said. "What do you do, if I may ask?"

"I work for ADI Holdings as an assistant. It's boring, and it doesn't challenge me, but it pays for as much graduate school as I care to attend."

"What're you studying?"

"Finishing an MBA, thinking about law school."

Emily nodded, clearly impressed.

After that, the questioning of Gen seemed mostly to cease. No one pestered us about how we'd met. There was no cross-examination. Dani and Emily had invited me; I'd invited Gen. That's all anyone there needed to know and they were satisfied with it.

I ate whatever I wanted. After my third glass of Pumking I let go of counting calories. I still didn't eat any dessert; not because I was hanging on to my usual habits, but because I didn't have much of a taste for it anymore.

It was the best meal I'd had all year. It always was.

Chapter 19

I waddled outside to take a seat on the stone bench in the garden. Night fell. Gen sat down next to me. I saw her suppress a shiver and I immediately started to pull my sweater off, but she stopped me with her hands on my wrists.

I put my arm around her shoulders instead and she huddled against me.

"How'd I do," she murmured.

"Everybody likes you. Of course they do."

"Not sure about Danielle..."

"She's just protective. I'm sure when I meet your friends it'll be the same."

"I'm not sure I want to let you near any of my friends. They might try to steal you."

I laughed, but it felt like my lungs were full of stuffing, so it wasn't a big laugh. "They'd fail."

We were silent a moment. She breathed against my side. It felt like a moment to Say Something.

"Gen," I started, then stopped immediately. "I, uh. I'm not generally really good at...being happy. Knowing what it feels like or how to acknowledge it. Am I making any sense?"

"Why don't you just keep going and I'll let you know when you get to the end." There was a hint—just a hint—of laughter in her voice.

"I guess the point is I may not be *good* at being happy but I am. Right now. Very happy. Happy in ways I didn't really remember were possible."

She leaned in closer against me. I didn't know what kind of shampoo or body wash or perfume she wore, but I could still smell it through all the cooking and food and the fall outdoors on her skin. It was good: simple, clean, feminine, just a little bit floral.

"Still going?"

"I am very happy with you. When I am with you. I've been a lot happier the past couple of months than most of the preceding year."

"Me too. Except all that stuff about being usually miserable; I kind of like my life. But I like it better with you in it. Now, my turn to ask you a question."

"Sure."

"When we met, the first time, in my office, you sailed in like James Bond's American cousin. You had the most confident smile I'd ever seen. You were wearing an off-the-rack suit that you still made look good. You were full of fast talk for ADI's security."

"There's not a question there but if you want to keep complimenting me…"

"We've been dating for two months and that confident smile, that kind of confidence in general, that slick talk—you aren't that way around me. Not since our first date. Now, don't get me wrong…I like your earnestness. That you get flustered around me is cute. But so is confidence. Just curious what the difference is."

"Ah. Well, when I walked into that office, I was working. I had a goal, a role to play, a way to get there. That's how I am on the job, I guess, when I have to talk to people. A mask I can put on."

"And now that we're dating?"

I looked down at her. "This is me, darlin'," I said. "I'm a pretty good investigator and a pretty good cook and maybe not a whole lot else. But you tell me the parts you like and I'll work on getting better at them."

"Calling me darling is a good start," she said. She leaned up suddenly and kissed me, briefly, but it warmed me up through my toes.

"I'll keep that in mind."

I wanted to say something else, about leaving on Monday and how I didn't want to. I started to open my mouth, draw in the breath I'd use, and I think she knew what I was going to say.

"Shh. Just sit here, ok?"

I did exactly that until Dani came outside to start a fire in the firepit.

I got up to help her. Gen squeezed my arm and slipped back inside to warm up.

Dani was silent while we got the fire started. Finally, she spoke.

"I think today was your best work."

"The turkey or the duck?"

"All of it." She eyed me over the lit kindling, carefully set down a log. "You really like her."

"Yeah," I admitted. No point in pretense or prevarication with Dani.

"Look, Jack," she said, standing up and looking me square in the eye. "You're my best friend. I love you. So don't take what I'm about to say the wrong way."

I swallowed hard, but nodded.

"She likes you just as much. So don't fuck it up."

Chapter 20

I was up far too early Monday morning. It was gray and drizzly, which was fine, because that matched my mood as I sped down Route 1 to Dover. At least I was beating rush hour. I wasn't thrilled about the way my gym bag was bouncing along on my back, weighed down with my spare clothes and the vest my boss had forced on me.

I was even less thrilled with the Tazer on my belt and the gun under my arm, but least I was keeping it unloaded. For now.

I could live with the baton Dani had slipped me. That felt a little better than the other weapons I was carrying. More personal. More honorable, somehow. I'd managed to fit the sheath along the back of my belt where a shirt could hang over it, and I'd spent yesterday practicing quickly drawing it and snapping it open.

If the moment came that I did have to use it, I was pretty sure I could surprise the heck out of whatever villain needed his arm broken.

I tried to think about the job as I rode, and not what I was leaving behind. Gen and happiness. I wasn't used to feeling the way I had the past few weeks. I hadn't even spent Sunday punishing myself for eating on Saturday. Emily and Dani had insisted we take their guest room that night, and we'd spent Sunday doing couples stuff. Walking the boardwalk in Havre de Grace while the wind blew around us and rain threatened without ever falling. Window shopping. There'd been some minor talk about Christmas and what we might be doing then. Nothing definite.

But it made a man want to go out and buy some lights to decorate his boat with. Not that I ever entered the *Belle* in any contests, or joined any of those lit boat parades. Then again, maybe I would this year. Who knew what the next month might bring?

Once I got off the highway I dutifully followed the GPS directions over my helmet's Bluetooth speaker to the parking lot of a chain hotel. I saw a big motor coach, two vans, and a long trailer all assembled, a few people milling around them.

I pulled up to a few stares. The roadies looked unimpressed; I could pick them out because they were either smoking or loading bags on the bus or the vans, or rolling boxes on to the trailer. Or both. It seemed like talent and support staff were just standing around.

I revved the engine a little unnecessarily as I guided It into a parking spot. I swung off the saddle carefully, adjusting my gym bag.

I saw one of the security guys I'd seen back in Wilmington. "Mr. Gogarty around?"

He laughed a little. "You think the owner comes out to see the company off? Maybe break a champagne bottle over the bus?"

"Well, if not him, who do I talk to? I'm hired help."

He took a long look at me. "You new talent?"

"No. Private security for an employee."

"Better talk to Ms. Stein," he said, jerking a thumb over his shoulder. "She'll be on the bus, staying warm."

"Thanks."

No point in being timid about it. I headed right for the bus door, knocking as I climbed up the steps. As buses went, it was the luxurious kind. It had about half as many seats as it could have, and most of them were arranged in pairs around tables, and all had space to recline. It was about a third full regardless, mostly of hulking presences in winter jackets and sweatshirts. I felt distinctly out of place, unwanted, like I'd just intruded into some kind of sacred space.

The darkness inside it was a noted contrast even to the muted late fall morning light outside, so I squinted from the top step. "Ms Stein? I was told to speak with you."

"You must be Dixon." A form from the back of the bus disengaged from a group in conversation and moved up the center aisle.

"Yes ma'am," I said, as Daphne the ring announcer came into focus. She was wearing a puffy red vest over a gray sweatshirt, jeans tucked into boots that almost reached her knee. Her hair was pulled back into a pony tail underneath a brown leather flat cap that you usually saw on Irish or Scottish shepherds on PBS.

She gestured to the door and I backed out, then a few paces away from the door. She walked around the other side of the bus, getting us as much privacy as we were likely to find.

"I don't want you on my bus," she said flatly as soon as I joined her. It wasn't a great place to start our working relationship. "The bus is for talent and creative and support only if they can't fit in the damn vans."

I was preparing my rebuttal when she held up a hand to stop me.

"However, Mr. Gogarty isn't giving me much of a choice. He says you go wherever Grant goes."

"That is my mandate, ma'am."

"Do I look like a ma'am to you?"

"Absolutely," I said, but with a smile, a little wattage in it, a little appreciation. "But I can stick with Ms. Stein if you prefer."

"Hrm." She cracked a smile. I was moving up in her estimation. "You got gear to stow?"

"Just this bag," I said, patting it. "And what's on my back. You should know that I am armed, under instructions from my employer."

"With what?"

I unzipped my jacket and held the left side out, showing the pistol under my arm. Then I pulled back the right and showed the Taser.

"Don't go shooting anyone at any of my shows."

"Wouldn't dream of it, Ms. Stein. I don't like carrying a firearm, and I doubt very much that I'll need to use it."

"Good. What do you need from me?"

"Well, to be honest, the company's been pretty slow giving me information. I've seen a copy of a threatening letter, and been sent a document that scraped together a lot of negative comments on various wrestling-related message boards and blogs. But I haven't seen much more than that."

"Well," Daphne said, rolling her eyes a little, "if you ask me, there isn't a whole lot to see. But there have been some calls, and Mr. Gogarty is worried."

"Are there any recordings of these calls? Transcripts, at least?"

"Not that I've heard."

"You think there's anything behind these threats, then?"

"Doesn't matter what I think."

"It does if you're the straw boss while we're on the road. I'm protecting Grant, but I'm answering to you."

"I'll say this much. Talent that gets fans angry is good, because anger is still engagement. But fans actually threatening that talent? Much less attacking it? That'd be bad as hell for business."

I wasn't entirely sure that was true; I could see how a foiled attack could generate some real coverage. But I wasn't about to say that.

"I'll do whatever I've got to do to make sure that doesn't happen, Ms. Stein. I do have one question when it comes to gear storage, however."

"And that is?"

"It might be convenient, or even necessary, for me to have my own means of transportation at my disposal."

"So rent a car."

"I have to be next to Grant most of the time. But might there be room on the trailer for a bike?"

She rolled her eyes and said, "Show me."

* * *

The roadies weren't happy about it, but Daphne insisted they carve out space for It on their trailer. In truth it wasn't even that hard to do; there was plenty of space and It wasn't a large bike.

I wasn't about to take their goodwill as a given, though. Once it was on, I picked out one of the crewmembers and waved him over. "Who's the loadmaster?"

"Eh?"

"Who's in charge of the stuff on the truck?"

He pointed to a man standing a few yards away. He wore an old Army field jacket, a tattered black watch hat, jeans, and Converse. I tapped him on the shoulder. A face with the tale of mileage and years turned around to me.

I stuck out my hand. "Jack Dixon. I'm the guy whose bike is taking up space on your truck."

His grip was like iron. "Braddox," he said. "Your bike is a pain in my ass."

"I understand that. Which is why I'm offering considerations to make sure it stays in good shape."

"What kind of considerations?"

"Twenty bucks for every day it has to take up space. A case of beer or a bottle of whiskey every time it has to get unloaded or loaded back up."

"Thirty and one of each."

I shook my head. "Pick one of those two."

He frowned. "It's gonna be in the trailer every damn day on this tour. Thirty bucks a day is gonna add up."

"Not if I deal with my business before this is over." In truth, compared to what I would make for being here, and being on the clock twelve, maybe sixteen hours a day, thirty dollars a day felt like I was getting off cheap.

"We'll take the booze, then. Never goes amiss."

"Alright. But if we wind up in a dry town I don't want that held against me."

He grinned. "Your phone'll always tell you where the county line is."

"True. Company doesn't have any prohibitions against drinking on tour, do they?"

Braddox laughed. It sounded like rocks and marbles being rolled together in a dice cup, and it smelled like coffee and cigarette smoke being wafted in my face. "Son, any outfit tries to tell us not to drink is gonna be looking for new crew. So long as we can pack and unpack the truck, nobody cares what the fuck we drink. Or smoke. Or chew. Nobody in my crew snorts or shoots anything till tour's over, though. Braddox's rules. You're wired, you're fired."

"Good to know."

"How 'bout a down payment?"

"Thought we agreed on booze."

Braddox shrugged.

I slipped out my wallet and dropped three tens into his gnarled hand. They disappeared faster than an old hand when a Chief Petty Officer was putting together a shit detail.

I was pretty sure I could work with this Braddox. I just hoped they didn't beat It to hell for being a foreign object on their truck.

Chapter 21

The buses didn't actually pull out until almost ten o'clock. I should've known that would be the case. People were late; people milled around. Gear wasn't packed the way the crew wanted it. There were some minor squabbles over seating arrangements. I was happy to find plenty of legroom where I sat down next to Grant.

Either he didn't rate one of the table seats or he hadn't wanted one. Regardless, I was delighted to find USB chargers on the back of the seats in front of me, and wifi on the bus. Grant was tired, red-eyed, and not talkative, so I got my tablet out and my earbuds in.

Surprisingly I had an email that wasn't work or spam related. Instead, it was from Gen, a link to a streaming playlist titled "Bus Music."

I clicked on it and leaned back in the chair, wondering what she had in store. When the first notes, and then the first lyrics hit, I knew I was listening to a cover of Simon & Garfunkel's "America." It was First Aid Kit, one of her favorite bands. By the time the closing notes sounded, I was clicking repeat.

It was a beautiful song, and I wasn't sure the version by these Swedish sisters wasn't better than the original. It was the perfect song to start a bus trip with, naturally.

I already missed Gen more than I would care to admit.

* * *

When Grant stirred himself to wakefulness, I slipped my earbuds out and turned off the music in order to signal my availability to chat.

"This is exciting, yeah man?" Grant woke up all at once. He went from muzzy-eyed sleep to bright-eyed talkative best pal in the blink of an eye. I mistrusted that.

"It's a nice bus, but I'm not real sure where we're going."

"Ocean City, man! The shore!"

"Jersey or Maryland?"

"Maryland."

"Then it ain't the shore. Ocean City Maryland is 'down e' Ocean,'" I said, affecting a Baltimore accent. "Remember, you're dealing with a native here."

Grant laughed a little and turned around in his seat. "Hey, everybody, we got a real native Baltimorean here, gonna teach us how to talk like one," he called out.

I wished real hard for the ability to blend in with the seat, or to disappear entirely. It wasn't forthcoming. Maybe I could kick a hole in the floor of the coach and hurl myself at the wheels.

"Grant," I muttered, "let's try and be a little bit lowkey about this arrangement, huh?"

He sat back down, disappointment on his face, like a kid who's been told the ice cream flavor he wanted is gone. "You gotta loosen up, Jack."

"Look, the fewer people that notice me, the better off we are. The easier it is for me to do my job."

"Fine, fine. We'll go all top secret if that's what it's gotta be. So how'd you wind up doing this PI stuff anyway?"

"After the Navy, I was a cop for a little while. Didn't like that too much, so I went looking for jobs that offered a little more freedom. Wound up working for a firm in Maryland, not all that far from where I grew up."

"So as a PI you're what, basically a private cop? Do all the same stuff but none of the red tape?"

"Not even close." This was the last thing I wanted to talk about, but doing so might draw him out on the threats and who might be angry at him. "I don't do nearly the same kind of stuff, and I have no arrest powers and no right to ruin anyone's day."

"That sounds like it kinda sucks, dude."

"I spend a lot of time following assholes who are cheating on their wives."

"Kind of a buzzkill. You do any cool stuff as a cop?"

I almost asked what he meant by cool stuff, but I assumed he meant high speed chases, shootouts, drug busts, undercover stings.

"Mostly I asked people for their fishing licenses and wrote tickets if they didn't have one or it was expired."

"Fishing licenses?"

"I was Department of Natural Resources Marine Police. Boat cop."

"Didn't even know they had those."

"Maryland's got a lot of waterway, lot of boaters. Gotta have cops."

"Huh. Pretty sweet to be out on the water all day, right?"

"For every day on the water I spent at least a day in an office filling out paperwork. And in winter when the waterways become more or less impassable, I spent every day inside. Wasn't for me." I hoped my tone told him to stop asking about it.

"Gotcha, gotcha," he said, his head nodding. Didn't seem he had at all. I took the initiative when he lapsed into silence.

"So what can you tell me about these threats?"

"Well, Gog forwarded you the emails, right?" He pronounced it with a long *o*. I wondered how his employer felt about that.

"I got a couple emails, yeah. One had a scan of a letter. The other was just a bunch of links to some comments on message boards and blogs."

"Those were threats too, man!"

"If everybody who made a threat on a message board was serious, every detective in the world would be working overtime to book them. If there was a pattern of someone on your social media sending you threats, making specific claims, showing knowledge of your work or your home…that'd worry me. That'd be actionable. But a bunch of internet handles on wrestling boards, just saying that they don't like your character or your style? That's not a lot to go on."

"Well, there are the calls."

"Alright. Tell me about the calls." I reached into a pocket of my jacket and pulled out my little metal-cased notebook and pen, opened it, got ready.

"The calls come after shows. Always directly to my hotel room."

"Okay." I wrote as he spoke. "Go on."

"They tell me to abandon the character. That it's offensive to the honor of the south, you know?"

"Yeah, I know," I said, weighting my words with as much scorn as they could hold. "But what do they say?"

"The last one said if I ever do the gimmick in Virginia again, that I should be prepared to pay with my soul. Whatever the hell that means."

"How do they know to call *your* hotel room?"

"Look, man, the venues we play, the towns we're in? It's not like there's that many options. Pretty easy to just look and figure out where the bus is parked."

"Yeah, that narrows it down, but how many rooms does this company book every night? Forty, fifty?"

"Yeah, something like that. So you call the front desk and say you're 'Grant's friend' and the guy puts you through. It ain't like A Squad is on duty at 2 a.m."

"So the calls come at 2 a.m.?"

"I dunno, I just pick up the phone. I don't put my contacts in to look at the clock."

I made a note of the contacts. You never knew what might be important later.

"Well, I'm gonna be rooming with you. The phone rings and you are not absolutely expecting a call on the hotel line, I'm answering it. You got me?"

"Absolutely," he said, "absolutely."

"Good. Now…these calls, how many have there been?"

"I dunno. Five, six?"

"Always when you're in Virginia?"

"Maybe in Maryland, too."

"Okay. Is it always after a *show* in Virginia? Maybe you performed in Virginia and then drove to Maryland, or even Pennsylvania, overnight, and got the call then?"

"Uh, I dunno. Probably not."

"So it feels pretty local. How many venues in Virginia have you played?"

"Couple in Richmond, down in Norfolk, Newport News, Virginia Beach, Williamsburg…"

"Okay, so a lot of towns," I said. "We'll worry about narrowing it if it happens again. How many dates are scheduled for this run?"

"We got three shows a week right up until Christmas. Couple days off for that back in Dover, then we go on the road again through January."

"Well, let's hope your stalker shows himself right away and we wrap this up right quick," I said. I'd winterized the *Belle* just in case, and paid Marty through the end of the year for my rental space and the extra we arranged for my hookups, even though I wouldn't be using them. But who wanted to live out of a gym bag for that long?

"So is there a show tonight?"

"Nah, but there will be a meet and greet at the hall. First night of a tour you don't get out there and do the whole show. Everybody's gotta settle in. Maybe we'll cut some promos for the website, or for tomorrow night…"

"Cut a promo?"

"Talking shit into the camera about the other guy," Grant interpreted. "Pretty basic stuff, man. Don't you know anything about pro wrestling?"

"Look, the last time I really paid attention to wrestling, I was a kid and The Rock was just becoming famous for it. I didn't think much about the terminology."

"Man, that's a while ago now. You never kept up with it?"

"I discovered that girls did not, in fact, have cooties. And that lots of research was required to prove it."

Grant laughed, thankfully. I wasn't entirely sure how the rest of the bus might have taken that. I'd have to tone that kind of stuff down.

"Bet you were a real slayer..."

"Not so much. Wrestling wasn't exactly a glory sport in Baltimore prep school circles in my day. If you didn't play football or lacrosse you might as well play nothing."

"I hear that. Out in Iowa it's football, football, football."

"Let's get back to the threats," I said. "Can you remember exactly what's said?"

"Man, I told you what I can remember."

"Well, look. Think on it. Think back to the calls you've gotten. Think on exactly what is said. How it's said. What the voice sounds like. Accents. Speech patterns. You never know what might be important."

"Alright, man. I'll think on it."

"You think of any detail, any detail at all, you tell me."

"Will do." He pursed his lips for a moment. "Wonder when we're gonna stop for lunch."

That seemed to be as much as I could get out of him. Dutifully I opened up the firm's app on my tablet and started entering the info I had, such as it was.

It turned out that we stopped for lunch pretty quickly, and not all that far from our destination. The bus and the vans pulled into the parking lot of a Denny's. Fast food restaurant signs were visible down the street.

"I can definitely use a couplea burgers," Grant said. "What about you?"

I thought about the six jars of almond and peanut butter in my gym bag. "How about Denny's?" At least in there I could eat eggs and other proteins and live with myself if I didn't get to a gym. "Their burgers are pretty good." I couldn't believe my own lies, but Grant bought it.

"I guess. Can always have 'em put an egg on top of it."

* * *

An hour later, full of bitter coffee, overcooked eggs, and greasy bacon, we went through the laborious process of checking into our hotel. When we did, Daphne pressed an envelope of cash into everyone's hand. Mine held three wrinkled ten dollar bills: my per diem. Every dollar of which I was going to be handing over to the roadies, more than likely. Once I'd let Braddox get thirty bucks out of me and a promise of booze, it was all over. But in the end it'd be a small price to pay to keep It in good condition.

There looked likely to be a lot of standing around here. We stood around in the parking lot after eating. We stood around outside the hotel to get room assignments. We stood around inside to get per diem. I tried to make myself useful, staying glued to Grant's hip and looking at everyone but him.

I doubted that these threats were coming from any of his fellow performers, or the rest of the folks in the company. But doubt was not investigative certainty, and I figured the first task I had to perform was to rule out everyone that was around Grant.

Hell, I thought. Imagine if this is just a prank by another wrestler that got way out of control.

That idea was appealing. Probably too appealing; it led to a quick resolution and minimized the possibility of any real threat. And thinking of it reminded me that I probably did need to try and interview the other wrestlers. The question there, as I saw it, was whether to go about that quietly or officially. Quietly would take longer but be more reliable. Officially, I could probably knock it out in a couple of days of sitting around a hotel conference room.

But that depended on everyone's cooperation. And goodwill from management. Based on the looks I'd gotten since I'd arrived—and the fact that no one had sat down to eat with me and Grant—seemed unlikely.

Guess I was doing it the hard way.

Chapter 22

Once we were checked into a big chain motel, Grant didn't show much motivation to do anything except sit on his double bed and flip channels.

I settled on the other one and tried not to look at the television. I'd lived so long without one that I found the experience of channel flipping dizzying, even nauseating.

"You got any meetings today? Walk-throughs? Story development?"

"Eh, maybe." He flipped from one sports-related talking-head show to another. It didn't look like an improvement.

"What do you mean, maybe? Do they give you schedules? Agendas?"

"Probably in my email."

"Forward it to me, then, would you?"

Reluctantly, Grant tore his eyes from the screen and dug out his phone. After a few seconds of flipping, my own buzzed.

I got out my tablet and popped open his agenda. According to it, he had a call at the arena at 3 p.m., just about ninety minutes from now.

"How early do you need to be at the arena for a 3 p.m. call?"

"They'll call me here and someone'll drive me over."

"Where's everybody else?"

"Probably either in their rooms, in the hotel gym, or at the arena."

I decided it probably wasn't my place to offer any career advice but I imagined that being in the gym or at the arena was the way to get ahead.

"Well, we're going over there early."

"How?"

"Walking. How far can it be, a few blocks?"

"Is that safe?"

"You're supposedly under threat in Virginia, not Maryland. And I want to get the lay of the land if we're gonna be here for two nights. Come on; get dressed however you need for whatever you've got to do there."

Grant shut off the TV, rolled off the bed, and began rooting around in his suitcase.

"You ever think about getting in the ring?"

"Absolutely the fuck not."

"You were good, Jack."

"Yeah, at…" I struggled for words that weren't 'real wrestling.' "At the collegiate, freestyle stuff. Not what you're doing."

"It translates, though. Lot of the same movements, same muscle use."

"I'm not in that kind of shape anymore."

"Oh, please," Grant said, as he took off his jeans and replaced them with sweats. "Couple of months in the gym, find the right supps, eat chicken and beans every meal, you'd be ready to go."

I didn't ask exactly what the right 'supps' were because I was pretty sure I wouldn't like the answer.

"C'mon," I said, gesturing towards the door after he'd pulled a t-shirt on and grabbed his jacket. "Let's go."

Down in the lobby we ran into one of the staff security guys and Daphne. The latter waved Grant over to her, which I quickly realized was a tactic meant to give the security guy some time to talk to me. It was the same guy who'd let me back the night of the show.

He barred my way with a hand planted on my chest. I didn't much like that, but I also didn't see any reason to start much of a tussle over it.

"Don't think I like some rent-a-cop walking around my sets with a gun," he said.

"Good thing I'm a rent-a-*detective*, then."

He sneered at me. "What's the difference?"

"I'm more expensive."

"Hah. Hah. You ain't wearing a piece on my sets."

I sighed. "What's your name?"

"Shawn, but you can call me sir."

"Shawn," I said, "let me be real clear. I don't like carrying a gun. But what I like even less is the idea of handing over a gun that's *known to the authorities* to be in my possession over to someone I don't know from Adam. And I'm not about to leave it sitting in a motel room. Safest place for it to be is on my belt, so that's where it's gonna stay."

"We'll see about that." I saw that Grant had picked up on whatever kind of pecking order bullshit that was being thrown at me and he quickly stepped over and put a hand between me and Shawn.

"C'mon, boss, leave my man alone," he said to the security chief. "He's gotta stay with me."

Shawn gave Grant a considering eye but then nodded. I brushed past him—gently. I wasn't particularly interested in starting a fight with anyone, much less someone I would've preferred to work with.

On our way out the door, I shot a look at Daphne. "You ever try and separate me from Grant again—even for thirty seconds—and the first goddamn thing I'm doing is calling your boss and becoming the biggest pain in the ass he's ever had. And believe me, I can be a *world class* pain in the ass."

The smirk she'd been wearing turned into a kind of shock. I think that people in the orbit of the DWF did not usually speak harshly to Daphne Stein.

With that, I grabbed Grant and marched him out the front door.

Chapter 23

The walk to the arena was short, but the weather was brisk enough to cool me down. Grant didn't seem to know what to make of what had gone on, so I took it upon myself to explain.

"Your company's security guy doesn't like that I'm here. He wanted to establish an order, see if he could push me around. Daphne maybe put him up to it. If they try it again, I'm gonna have to get loud about it."

"I wouldn't, man. Shawn is kind of a scary dude."

"That so?"

"Yeah. Army Ranger, ex-cop. Says the money's better in private security."

"Well, here's hoping we don't have to find out what's what." I wasn't too worried. My guess was that Shawn had fewer options and more scruples than I did if it came to some kind of fight. But I still wasn't looking for one.

The arena turned out to be a pretty nondescript event space—the kind that would host most any kind of mid-sized performance. Anything from ballet to theater to political rallies to, apparently, wrestling. The theater's sign indicated that DELMARVA WRESTLING FEDERATION was in town for ONE NIGHT ONLY, featuring Derrick Rigg and Spitfire.

From the little I'd seen, those two certainly deserved to be the headliners. Nothing was going on in it tonight. In the central amphitheater it looked like the ring was under construction, with roadies testing the ropes and smacking the canvas.

I followed Grant into the backstage area, where he began exchanging greetings with familiar figures. I saw Blake, wearing a plain gray sweat suit and smelling faintly of Icy Hot.

"You're here early," he said, with no small amount of surprise in his voice.

"Yeah, well." Grant gestured at me.

Blake reached and shook my hand. "Are you here to instill a work ethic in our boy while keeping him safe?"

"Well, life-coaching usually costs extra. But with the right retainer, I can roll it into the standard Elite Protection package."

Blake snorted. Grant didn't seem to get the joke, or if he did, he didn't much like it. His face clouded and he said, "Well, now that I'm here early, what am I gonna do?"

"Stretch," Blake said, "then get in the ring and we'll block some stuff out. Practice a little."

"Fine, fine," Grant said. "I gotta hit the bathroom." He looked at me. "You don't have to follow me there, do ya?"

I sighed. "I should probably stand outside." I followed him down the hall and so did Blake. When Grant went in and shut the door, I turned to him.

Time to start unofficially questioning the company, I guess.

"Grant not usually one for early work?"

He shrugged. "It's the boring stuff."

"Being willing to do the boring stuff is usually what makes someone good at something."

"No," he corrected me, "it's what separates good from great."

"Fair. So…you heard anything about the threats?"

He shrugged. "I don't pay attention to anything going on outside the ring. Just here to wrestle."

"Well, how do folks feel about Grant?"

Here, Blake frowned a little under his mustache. I was probably asking him to break some kind of backstage omerta.

"He's a little stiff," he said.

"Stiff?"

His frown deepened. "It's easier to get hurt working with him than with other wrestlers."

"I got it," I said. Just then, the bathroom door opened and Grant came out, wiping wet hands on his pants.

"Let's get to it," Blake said.

Chapter 24

I stood ringside while Blake and Grant walked through the match they would have the next day. It looked pretty similar to the one I'd seen. They went through it at a walking speed, without using any moves; nobody went off the ropes, nobody got picked up. They just walked to spots and gripped each other where they'd need to in the real match.

I noted that Blake did most of the talking. A couple of times, he adjusted Grant's hand placement or his stance.

I didn't think Grant liked being corrected, but I noticed something important; every time Blake corrected him, he did what was asked without a word. His feet shifted, he moved his hands, he changed his stance.

Grant might be the guy who was going to win the match, but Blake was definitely running it.

When they'd finished the slow speed walk-through, they did it again, half speed. Blake and Grant both bounced off the ropes a couple of times. Then they sped it up again, with Blake calling out moves, telling Grant when to duck or to roll.

They still avoided any big hitting stuff; nobody went up on the ropes and when either of them picked the other up or put on some kind of hold, I could see it wasn't done with any kind of intent.

I was reasonably sure I could cross Blake off the list. This guy seemed to be exactly what he presented himself as: a pro wrestler who just loved to work and wanted to make Grant better. I wrote a note to myself to check out Blake's history online later.

All told their walkthrough took over an hour. As they were wrapping it up I felt someone sidle up behind me.

I peeked over my shoulder and saw Daphne. "Ms. Stein."

"Mr. Dixon. I'm not used to being spoken to that way on the road."

"I'd prefer not to piss you off. But I've got a job to do."

"Understood. In fact, I found it a bit refreshing. The talent all walk around on eggshells around me. And it seems like you're serious about your work."

"I am," I replied. "It's maybe the only thing I'm serious about." Besides the squat rack and Geneva Lawton, I thought. But there was no call to go telling Daphne that.

"Good. Grant's got some real talent," she said. "If he can work hard enough to harness it, he could be something in this business."

That was the second time someone had commented negatively on Grant's work ethic. That was an emerging pattern. I was a detective. Nothing like that was going to slip by me.

"What's he got to work on?"

"Everything," Daphne said flatly. "In the ring, on the mic, in the weight room. Everything," she repeated.

"I see." A pause. "How long's he been with the company?"

"This is his second time on the road with us as a full-timer. He'd been pulled in on short contracts a couple of times; auditions, essentially."

"So why'd you take him on if you don't think he works hard enough?"

"I didn't. Gogarty did."

"Ah." Daphne didn't have hiring or firing power. I made a note.

"Look, I still think the guy has a lot of potential. But if he doesn't learn to love the work by thirty, he's never going to."

I held back my own thoughts on what an employee owed an employer. From where I stood 'loving the work' usually meant 'putting it above everything you actually loved in some misplaced show of loyalty.' But there was no need to get into that with someone whose good side I needed to be on.

"So, look. Ms. Stein. I hate to have to ask these questions, but…is there anyone with the company who might wish Grant harm?"

She shook her head. "I don't think so. And if they did, all they'd have to do is asked to be booked with him and run a shoot."

"What a what?"

"A shoot is when you hurt somebody in the ring. On purpose."

I looked up from my notebook. "That happens?"

She laughed. "You take a dozen or more hyper competitive people, all used to being the alpha? Throw them together on the road, with the pressures of schedules and performance and audience reaction, and everybody's competing for a limited amount of heat? Of course they'll try to hurt each other."

"I'm sorry. Heat?"

"Audience reaction. Buzz. Heat is how you move up. Generate enough of it and bigger companies take notice…"

"So your wrestlers look at DWF as just a step-ladder?"

"Works both ways," she said. She gestured with her chin at Blake, who was going over some kind of hand-positioning with Grant. "Blake there is on his way down. Making it last as long as he can."

"His way down?"

"He's been in this game a long time. Longer than me. Hell, I only fell into it because I never quite made it from stunt-work to acting, and even then I barely really wrestled. Being a chaperone and an announcer always fit me better anyway."

I nodded, tapping my pen against the notebook. What she was saying just now didn't seem all that useful, but you do enough investigating, you learn to give people the space to talk. Don't interrupt them and you never know what they might say.

"Anyway, Brian—that's Blake's real name—he's had his sniff of the bigtime. On big TV packages once or twice, been on the house shows before a pay-per-view, that kind of thing. Never quite broke through."

"That kind of thing could grate on a man," I muttered.

"Not Blake. He lives and breathes this business. So if the only work he can get is to job for a guy like Grant, he'll take it. And he'll still try to do it all the right way."

"Job?"

She laughed. "Do you know even one sentence of information about wrestling?"

"I know a lot about the collegiate game."

She turned to look at me, and reached out to poke my chest with one finger. I didn't have the vest on and my bike jacket was hanging open. Vanity demanded that I not let the side down, so I tensed up and her finger bounced off.

"That how you know Grant?"

"We were teammates."

"Ah, old college buddies. That why he wanted to hire you, huh? Do his old roommate a favor?"

"We were teammates," I said, in the same flat tone of voice I'd said it the first time. Daphne got the hint and laughed slightly.

"Well, if you're eliminating suspects, you can cross Brian off your list. He'd hurt himself in the ring to save whoever he was working with before he'd hurt them to make himself look good. It's just not in him."

I understood what she meant, and I was sure she believed it. I'd like to believe it, too. But everything she was saying only made me want to take a second and third look at Blake Irons.

"One more question," I said, as it looked like Blake and Grant were about finished, as they were slipping out of the ring and grabbing towels and water bottles.

She looked at me, cocking a sculpted eyebrow.

"I'd like to be able to talk to all the other wrestlers…at least the folks Grant has worked with, or might. Or those whose careers he has an effect on."

"That'd be all of them, then."

"Well, the more of them I can talk to, the better."

"It's not someone in the company making those threats."

"I'd like to agree with you," I said, "but it's my job to eliminate everyone who could be doing it in order to find the person who *is*. And I'd be a pretty piss poor detective if I didn't approach this methodically."

"I suppose I can understand that. I'll put out the word that talent should expect questions. What about the crew?"

I'm not real sure that your security chief could figure out how to use a computer, I thought, but didn't say. And I couldn't see how the roadies were a threat to anyone unless it was a bartender signaling last call.

"Let's start with the talent, and I'll keep an eye on the crew."

"Good luck with that."

"I'll take all the luck I can get."

Chapter 25

The rest of that day passed in utter stultifying boredom. After his workout in the ring, Grant spent some time in the trainer's room getting treatment, which mostly meant a rubdown and some ice. Blake—or Brian, I wasn't sure how to think of him now—got his usual mummy-in-ice treatment.

If that guy needed that much work just to do the walkthrough I'd seen I couldn't imagine how he was still really performing. But a breaking body could go a long way if the mind was determined enough. I decided not to interrupt that with any talking, but I did make a note of the trainer. He reminded me of every trainer and PT I'd seen in my high school and college days. Maybe a little older. In excellent shape, wearing a polo-shirt tucked into khakis, a belt holding various kinds of medical equipment around his trim waist.

Name tag said Malik. I knew better than to interrupt him while he worked, so I just made a note to try and catch him later.

I walked Grant back to the hotel and we sat around the room for a while, him flipping channels, me reading.

"What do you need to do in the morning?" I asked.

"Sleep, eat, rest for the show."

"You don't plan to work out in the morning?"

"I might like to get up a sweat before the ring. Blake's not a fan of oiling up, but the crowd usually likes the look, so sweat it is."

"I'm sorry, oiling up?"

"Yeah, you know. Put on baby oil. Makes the muscles look good under the lights."

"Right. Well, I need to get in a work out at some point. This hotel's got a gym, right?"

"Sure does."

"Want to go see what it's got?"

"Not really."

I sighed. "Look, if I leave you alone in here, do you promise... promise...not to go anywhere, not to pick up the room phone, and to call my cell if there's so much as a knock at the damn door?"

"Didn't you say you weren't supposed to get separated from me?"

"Not in public where anyone can see. Here in the hotel, I know exactly where you are. It's got pretty limited access in and out, so anyone intending to do you harm probably has to make themselves known to a camera or an employee at some point. In fact, I should probably do a walk around and find out how limited the access is."

"Probably?" For once, Grant stopped looking at the television and turned to me. "You don't sound real sure."

"I told you, I'm a detective, not a bodyguard. I have some ideas about what I'm supposed to do, but my best bet is to find the source of the threats as quickly as possible so you can go back to resting easy."

From what I had seen so far, Grant really didn't have any problem with resting easy even now. But there was no angle in saying that.

"Then I'm going to take a walk around the hotel and check out the fitness center. You stay put. You don't leave for any reason without calling me to come get you." I went to my gym bag and pulled out one of the small canisters of pepper spray Jason had given me. I tossed it to him.

He caught it, startled. "What's this?"

"Somebody kicks down the door, you point this at them—make sure the nozzle is pointing *away* from you—you press down on the trigger, and ruin their day."

"Pepper spray?" He immediately turned the business end towards his own eyes and held it up close to read it. "Oh man. Cool. Can I keep this?"

"No. If you don't have to use it, I want it back. And it's not a toy! You can blind yourself with that stuff if you're not careful."

"Fine, fine." He set it down on the nightstand and sat back heavily on the bed. I could tell from the way he kept looking at it that he was probably going to pick it back up as soon as I left the room.

"Don't make me regret handing that to you," I said as I shut the door behind me.

* * *

There is no architecture in the world more boring than that of the national chain motel. Just endless empty corridors with the same carpet, the same doors, the same paintings hanging at the junctions and elevators.

Where did they get those paintings? Who was the artist or studio supplying the Holiday and Red Roof Inns of the world with their art?

"The Bland School," I murmured. "The Visual Oatmeal Movement. The Don't Focus Too Muchers." I was pretty sure I could have done better than those, but they were good first efforts.

It was a pretty standard hotel block, with cameras pointed at all the entrances, fire doors, and long hallways. There wasn't anything I could do, individually, to beef up the security, except stay glued to Grant all the time.

He didn't seem too worried for a guy who was spending a lot of company money on a supposed threat to his life. And nobody seemed at all interested in the idea that any threats might be coming from within the company.

Eventually I found my way to the fitness room. I had been hoping for a gym with at least one rack.

I couldn't be that lucky.

Against a mirrored wall was a short row of treadmills. In a far corner, a rack held a selection of kettlebells next to a row of dumbbells, rising from fifteen pounds to fifty-five in each case. There were some rolled up mats in the back. In the closest corner there was a resistance band machine, the kind that I assumed was there to make people *feel* like they'd gotten a workout without having to deal with something like real weights.

"Gonna be tough to get a workout," I muttered.

"You wanna go in there, I'll show you how to use some of the equipment. After you give me that piece on your shoulder."

Down at the end of the corridor stood Shawn, the security guy, wearing three different layers of Under Armour and a towel over his shoulder.

I did not have time for this. I did not have any real desire for this.

But I figured I might as well get it over with all the same. I ducked into the room and shut the door behind me and pressed my back against the wall.

Sean came boiling through the door. I didn't wait and I wasn't in the mood to be fair. I kicked him in the back of the knee. Hard.

To his credit, he stumbled forward but didn't go down, and he turned quickly and immediately charged.

When his shoulder hit me and pushed me back up against the wall hard enough to blow out some of my breath, I began to wonder if I had miscalculated.

I was able to brace enough to not be completely breathless, and I started bringing my elbows down on his back as hard as I could. On the third blow I actually caught the point of my elbow on the back of his head, which hurt me as much as him, but he backed away, dazed.

I didn't feel any too good about it either and we stood facing each other for a moment.

"I don't fuckin' work for you," I spat. "And I don't need to take your orders."

He shook away whatever was clouding his eyes and lifted his hands, falling into a boxing stance. At least, boxing was how my brain categorized it; I didn't much know or care what kind of martial arts this guy might know. I did know that with my back against the wall, I was capable only of reacting, not acting. And that had to change.

I let my wrestling training take over. I got low, lunged forward, shooting for his legs. I'm sure a coach would've yelled at me about my form, but I got him to the ground regardless.

I was not aiming for the safe return mandated by the rules I'd wrestled under in college. He landed hard.

Not hard enough; unfortunately I didn't control him once we hit the ground. At least there I had as much chance to deliver blows as he did, and certainly I took some. I barely had time to register one good shot to his chin—most of which was deflected as he ducked into his shoulder—before he rolled me off and came back to his feet.

I scrambled to my feet and shot for his legs again, low and fast and hard. Down he went. I got my knee up into his chest and my arm over his throat, my other hand pinning his shoulder down. None of this would've been legal if there was a mat and a ref. But there wasn't.

This seemed to count a lot more.

"You can give up or you can go to sleep," I said, through gritted teeth. He tried to buck me off of him, and his knee bounced off my tailbone a couple of times, once on to my lower back. Thankfully he'd lost the combat boots and replaced them with sneakers. It hurt, but he was losing breath. About now the world was starting to go dark on him.

"Enough," he rasped, barely able to get the words out. "Enough."

I took my arm away from his throat and popped to my feet. I extended a hand to help him up. He didn't seem eager to take it.

"Come on," I said, "Get up, straighten yourself out, inflate your lungs." I pulled him back to his feet and he staggered over to the one of the pieces of resistance-wire bullshit this gym was festooned with.

I could feel my adrenaline draining. I did not have anything resembling real fight stamina left. He backed away and stumbled into the seat of the resistance machine.

"Why," I said, "are you so determined to get my gun?"

He looked at me with disgust in his features. "Mr. Gogarty told me to, uh, figure you out when the tour got started. He said to start by taking your gun."

"What the fuck," I said, startled.

"Look, all I know is what I was told to do. I tried. You win. You fucking cheated, but you won."

"How'd I cheat?"

"Kicking me in the back of the knee instead of taking me head-on? Fuckin' pussy. My bad knee too. Bastard's gonna swell up like a grapefruit."

I rolled my eyes and decided I would ignore his stupidity to get at the bigger revelation.

"Why would your boss agree to hire me, and agree that I should go armed, and then tell his head of security to disarm me, violently, if necessary?"

"Beats the shit out of me. I don't know how that old man thinks."

"You going to let it go now?"

"Hey, man, I followed his order. I tried you out. You're for real."

"Christ," I muttered, wiping sweat out of my forehead. "This is so goddamn stupid. You could've just come to talk to me, you know. Professional to professional. Let me know that your boss had second thoughts or wanted to check my damn references."

"Would've defeated the point."

"What was the point? Now if some shit does go down, both of us are less effective."

He frowned, and stood up. "I better go see Malik, get some ice. You need treatment?"

"I think it's gonna look really fucking stupid if we both show up to see the trainer saying we got hurt separately when we've clearly been in a fight."

"Eh, it happens," Sean said. "People get in fights on the road all the time. He'll stay quiet."

I waved him off. "You go. I'll ice myself up."

Gingerly, he extended his hand. "No hard feelings?"

I stared at his hand. A part of me, a competitive part, wanted to take his hand by the wrist and finish what I'd started. But that was adrenaline and anger talking. I took his hand, gently, and shook. "No hard feelings. From now on, maybe just talk to me."

Chapter 26

I grabbed a stack of towels from the fitness room—I wasn't going to call it a gym—and made my way back up to mine and Grant's room. Grant had fallen asleep in front of the TV. I gathered up the ice bucket and made three trips to the machine in the hallway in order to get enough for all the towels.

The elbow I'd connected to Shawn's skull was sending some warning signals. But my lower back was definitely in the lead for most painful spot on my body, where his kicks had connected. I stuck two towels, wrapped around ice, in the waistband of a pair of shorts and leaned back on them. I rested my elbow on another, and just placed the remaining one atop my head.

I read quietly until Grant woke up about forty minutes later. Some contemporary fantasy epic that really could've used more plot and less description of grass and animals, if you asked me, but it passed the time.

Grant woke up and took a long look at me, squinting. "What the hell happened to you?"

"Disagreement with someone. It's all settled. Don't worry about it."

"You get in a fight with somebody?"

"Yep."

"You win?"

"Yep."

"Good."

"Not really. Was still a waste of time for us both. Pretty dumb all around."

"Man, that was your problem back in college, too."

I lifted my eyes from the e-reader app and slid them to Grant. "What?"

"You think too much when you should just, you know, fight."

"Thinking too much is not a weakness."

"It is on the mat. You just have to act."

"I spent enough time on the mat, Grant. That's one thing I'd prefer not to think about."

He sat up straighter, frowning, and muttered something noncommittal. He was silent a moment.

"You ever talk to that guy?"

I looked at him again. I wasn't getting anywhere in my novel. "What guy?"

"You know, the guy…"

"David Rackham."

"Yeah. Him."

"I don't think he'd particularly want to talk to me, Grant."

"Don't know unless you try."

"Some things are destined to remain mysterious."

"If you say so."

Grant busied himself with his phone for a while, and I tried to immerse myself in escapism. Then a question occurred to me.

"Hey, when do we get our dinner money?"

"Our what?"

"Dinner money."

Grant laughed. "You already got it, pal."

"Thirty bucks a day for breakfast, lunch, and dinner?"

"You're getting thirty? Shit, when I went on my first full time tour last year I only got twenty."

"Usually I get expenses covered when I'm working," I said. It came out like I was pouting. I didn't like the sound of it, but there was no taking the words back now.

"Oh yeah? Steakhouses, bar tabs, nice hotel rooms?"

"No," I said. "More like gas, coffee, the occasional Wawa sub. I've expensed drinks and the like, but only because I'd had to go into a bar or restaurant and just sitting there without ordering is the fastest way to draw suspicion."

"Well, this is as glamorous as this gets," Grant said, gesturing to the bland room around us. "Get used to it."

"How'd you wind up here, Grant?"

He shrugged. "There's no money to be made as a wrestler any other way."

"Don't have to be a wrestler."

"Well, I could go back to my dad's soybean farm. That pays even less, for harder work. I tried to get a job as a gym teacher and a coach at some high schools back home but I didn't have the right degree and I wasn't going back to school for it."

"What'd you major in?"

"Communications. What was it you were majoring in?"

"Philosophy with a minor in classics."

"Man, the coaches hated that…"

"Yeah, coaches always hate it when a player is smarter than they are and not afraid to say so."

"They weren't all that bad, man."

I decided to keep my opinion to myself on that. In my entire history of wrestling, from middle school through college, there wasn't one single coach—not my dad, not anyone else—that I looked back on fondly. They'd made me who I was, sure.

But that wasn't necessarily a good thing.

Chapter 27

The show that night went off without a hitch. Grant's act got the crowd booing a little, but it seemed a good-natured booing, if I was any judge. Booing that was in on the joke. Technically it seemed like the match with Blake went better than the first time I'd seen it. More applause, more audience engagement.

Then again, I didn't pay as much attention to the match as I did to the crowd.

I was still watching the crowd and getting ready to head backstage before the next match started, when I felt a hand tap my shoulder.

I whirled around. I didn't quite go for my gun, but I'd be lying if I said I didn't tense up a little.

Instead it was the lightly bearded wrestling blogger I'd met back in Wilmington, after Grant had stuck the spotlight on me.

"Tommy Wilkerson," I said, pulling the name up from wherever I stored them.

"That's right," he said. "And you're here again. Long way to come to watch a match you've already seen."

"Yeah, well, I'm working." I turned to go.

"Working on what? Got your jacket all zipped up...looks kinda hot. And bulky. Somebody might think you were carrying a gun."

I turned on Tommy Wilkerson, who suddenly looked a lot cannier than I'd given him credit for.

"You put that together all by yourself?"

He shrugged. "I'm a journalist. It's my job."

You're a wrestling blogger, I thought. But it didn't seem wise to say. "You just keep your surmises to yourself, then."

"Hey, if there's something going on, I might be able to help you figure it out."

"In exchange for what?"

He shrugged. "Exclusives."

By then the house lights were going down and entrance music was starting up. I needed to get backstage. Tommy dug in a pocket and handed me a wrinkled and slightly damp business card, which I took reluctantly.

"Think about it," he said as I retreated.

* * *

I waited outside the clubhouse, which apparently was still strictly for talent only. Nobody—not Daphne, not Glen, not Shawn, not Grant—seemed willing to break whatever sacred prohibition was in place there.

I stood in the hallway listening to the crowd and hearing a little of the buzz in the dressing room. The door cracked open and Blake came hobbling out.

He was coated in sweat and looked like he needed help just to walk down the hall.

"You alright?" Instinctively I stuck a hand out but he waved it off and leaned against the opposite wall.

"I'll manage," he said. "I just don't have a lot left after time in the ring anymore, you know?"

"Seemed like it went better in there. Maybe working with Grant helps?"

He leaned back against the wall and closed his eyes for a long moment. "Kid could be good. Just gotta put the work in."

I neglected to point out that the kid was nearing thirty and that he'd been exactly like this when I'd known him in college.

"You know anything about the threats?"

Blake shook his head, eyes still closed. He was holding himself against the wall, back bent, hands on his knees. "I don't pay attention to anything but the show. I'm just here to wrestle. If you weren't here I wouldn't even know there'd been threats."

Slowly, Blake turned and, with one hand holding him up against the wall, walked down the hall.

Grant followed a bit after, carrying his vest and hat.

"What'd you think?"

"Crowd seemed to like it."

"You didn't watch?" He seemed crestfallen.

"I was watching the crowd," I said. "That's what you hired me to do."

"Fair." I followed him down the hall to where the treatment room had been set up. Blake was already stretched out on a table.

Grant waited for Malik's attention. When I went to stand by the table, the trainer waved me away.

"I gotta stay with my principal," I said.

"Well, you can stay in the room, but get the fuck away from my table," he said, without looking at me. He stretched out Grant's arm and said, "How's the elbow and the forearm? No pain?"

I decided that this was definitely not a fight worth picking and wandered a few feet away. Grant was ready a lot sooner than Blake was, and he led me to the monitors where the talent and backstage folks watched the action.

"Spitfire against Caliban," Grant said, pointing to the central monitor. The six foot and change redhead was absolutely dwarfed by her opponent—and it looked like she was the one doing all the work, flying off the ropes, swinging around him. He didn't seem to have much more going for him than a long reach and lunge, and a gigantic physical presence.

"Man, this stuff doesn't work," Grant muttered. "She's gotta do all the work and the crowd knows it. Not even sure why that guy is here."

We stood around and watched the rest of the show. There was no Rigg vs Spitfire and Night Witch match, but there was a lot of lead up to it, the interstitial stuff between matches seemed to focus on it.

All in all, the first night closed out quietly.

Then we went back to the hotel and got the letter.

Chapter 28

I was reading it for at least the fifth time, holding it with a plastic bag wrapped around my hand, pacing back and forth across the room. Grant sat on his bed, flipping his phone around in his hand nervously. Daphne sat on the other one, watching me pace. Finally, she cleared her throat.

I paused and turned to her in mid-step. "Yes?"

"Have you…" She waved a hand vaguely at the paper in my hand. "Detected anything?"

"Well," I said. "It's clearly a laser printer. I'd guess a Toshiba, made between 2006 and 2012 but I can't rule out later models. Written on a Mac, not a recent model. Typist was left-handed."

"Really?"

"No. That's all nonsense. It's just a piece of paper. I know exactly as much about it as you do."

She held out her hand. I shook my head.

"Nope. Not putting this in anyone's bare hands."

"Got a finger-printing kit in your gym bag, and access to an FBI database? Because otherwise, what's the point."

"If we progress to the point of a serious crime being committed, the police are going to want to see this."

"Aren't you here specifically to prevent that?"

"Yes, but I'm not perfect."

"Well you better be, because company policy is we don't call the cops unless it's a matter of life or death."

"That is not legally binding, and you know it."

"Look, Mr. Dixon," Daphne said, lowering her hand. "This is a top-down kind of culture. We circle our wagons and protect our own. That's why we hired you instead of going to the police. If your first instinct at the sign of trouble is to seek outside authority?" She tsked, shaking her head. "Maybe we've made a poor decision."

I decided to ignore her and read the letter again.

Grant Aronson,

We have warned you. We have told you. Perform this inflammatory act of desecration—spitting upon our sacred history and traditions— is unacceptable. Your ignorance of history and culture is no excuse. This aggression—unlike that of your gimmick namesake—will not stand. If you perform this routine in the sacred borders of Virginia, we will take action.

It was unsigned. I turned it over and looked at the envelope. It simply said "US Grant C/O Delmarva Wrestling." No address. No return address.

With a sigh, I folded it back up, placed it inside its envelope, and sealed it in another plastic bag. Let Daphne get indignant if she wanted; I wasn't going to go messing up potential evidence.

I tucked the sealed plastic bag into the back pocket of my jeans.

"The desk clerk wasn't too keen on answering any questions, but it seems like a fair amount of fan mail gets dropped off at the hotel every stop of the tour. At least that's what he said. That true?"

Daphne nodded. "It's a bit old fashioned, but yeah. People leave little gifts and letters such. Photos to sign if we're going to be in town two nights."

"Who do you know in the towns you play in Virginia?"

Grant shook his head. "Nobody, really. Nobody I can think of. Only person I know out east is you."

I studied him for a split second. He did not look worried. If anything he was grimacing, like he was trying to look worried and not sure how to go about it.

"The hotel's got a camera pointed at the front door," I said. "I can't compel them to let me see the footage. But maybe I can apply a little pressure." I looked at Daphne. "How would it go if I threatened that they might lose the DWF's business if they don't let me see it? That's about the only leverage I can come up with."

She nodded. "Sounds good."

"Fine," I said, waving to Grant. "Come on. We've got some video to watch."

"Hey, man, I haven't even had dinner yet."

I went to the luggage stand and unzipped my gym bag. I drew out a sealed plastic bag with cutlery and napkins, and then pulled out a pristine jar of my current favorite dinner: a creamy almond butter that cost far too much.

"You can share mine or order a pizza." I sighed. "Where's the nearest convenience store?"

"Ask your phone," Daphne said on her way out the door. "I've got shows to plan."

Chapter 29

Grant and I walked to the nearest gas station and procured some bottled cold brew coffee, milk, and yellow sweetener packets. He muttered something about a liquor store. As tempted as I was, it didn't do to mix a long boring job with alcohol.

He grabbed a bagful of junk food, and we made our way back to the hotel. I had to ring the bell twice to get the desk clerk—a young guy, scrawny and with a patchy beard—to come shuffling out from the little office behind the desk. He looked at me through grease-speckled glasses.

"Help you?"

"I'm with the DWF," I said.

"The what?"

"The wrestling company that's taking up half the rooms in your establishment right now." I leaned forward. "And I need to look at the front-desk security tape from today."

He blinked behind his glasses, taking them off to rub the bottom of his shirt ineffectually against them. When he put them back on the grease was, at least, more evenly applied.

"I, uh, don't know if I have the authority to let you do that."

"You have as much authority in this life as you give yourself... Kevin," I said, having paused just long enough to read his name-tag, which was similarly spattered with the detritus of whatever fast food he'd had for dinner. "Seize it. Grasp it with both hands. Don't let anyone take it away from you."

"Uh. Okay."

"Great," I said. An investigator's rule; when it seems even for a second like you're getting the answer that grants you access to something you probably shouldn't have, proceed full steam ahead. Redline the engine. Make the boilers glow as you shovel coal into them. I pointed to the doorway that led behind the desk. "Meet you back there?" I started walking, dragging Grant behind me with one hand.

By the time we were around the other side of the desk, Kevin clearly had no idea what to do or what he was dealing with. I wasn't necessarily above using a little physical intimidation if I had to, but Kevin looked like he went about six-foot-one and one-forty, soaking wet. It would've been like yelling at a puppy.

He led us to a small nook with a computer set on a folding table. The monitor, once he woke it up with a shake of the mouse, showed live feeds of the various cameras scattered around the hotel.

He pulled out the rolling desk chair and minimized the live feeds, then went to a folder marked "Cameras" and rooted around in it for a while.

"Okay," he said. "The last eight hours of the front desk should be in that file," he said, pointing to a QuickTime icon in a subfolder labeled FRONT, with today's date. "Good luck, I guess."

He left, then suddenly stuck his head back in. "Uh. Maybe don't tell the manager I let you do this?"

"Aren't you the manager, Kevin?"

"I'm the assisting night desk supervisor," he replied.

"Man's gotta have goals, Kevin. You think like a manager, act like a manager, tell yourself you're a manager, and someday it'll be true."

I gestured Grant into another seat, set my almond butter and my coffee down on the desk, and started fast forwarding through footage.

Movies and TV tend to gloss over just how mind-numbing—and how unlikely to help—going through security tape is. Sure, in the case of a stickup or a bank robbery, provided the perpetrator is dumb enough not to take any steps, it can easily lead to breaks in the case. And if an area is blanketed with closed circuit cameras like some places are, a criminal is almost guaranteed to give away some kind of helpful detail.

But the cameras at this particular hotel were not state of the art high-definition, nor were there an abundance of them. The camera sat right behind the desk and did show the faces of people who stopped and stared into it—but if an employee stood in the wrong place it would easily block the sightline.

I fast forwarded until any activity came along. It was so seldom my thumb started to get a friction burn. Eventually I would let up on the keys in order to eat a careful spoonful of almond butter.

Grant had blown through his entire bag of jerky, string cheese, chips, popcorn, and pork rinds by the time I was eating a third spoonful.

"Man, are you really just eating peanut butter for dinner?"

"Almond butter," I said. "And on a normal day it's what I eat for two, maybe three meals a day. I mean, not always this particular brand. But it's one of my favorites."

"Damn dude. Are you measuring it?"

He'd caught me in the act of scraping the excess out of the spoon I was using against the side of the jar.

"Helps me count the calories."

"Jeez. What are you training for? A Spartan race or something?"

"You know, the Spartans lost more wars than they won? They pretty routinely got their ass kicked. That their reputation is what it is today just goes to show you what good PR will do for you."

He laughed and said, "Hell yeah. PR is the wrestling business, bro. The more you can get people talking about you, the better every match is gonna be."

I stopped the playback and turned to him. "That so?"

He nodded.

"Then why the hell not report this to the cops?"

"I told you, man," Grant said. "Nobody wants cops crawling around them much."

"Look. I get that most of the road crew are probably holding. What about the talent?"

"You know," he said with a shrug. "Everybody needs a little pick me up, something to ease the pain…something to make workout recovery easier. Something to keep you in the ring."

"PEDs."

"Man," Grant spoke in a hushed whisper. "Don't say that the fuck out loud."

"You on anything, Grant?" I set down my almond butter. "This might be relevant later."

He let out a little sigh. "I cycled down before the tour started, okay? You know how fuckin' hard it is to stay in this kind of shape?" Then he waved a hand vaguely at me. "You telling me you keep those arms without any gear? Not even a few T patches now and then?"

"My use of pharmaceuticals is solely restricted to the kind that help me calm down and sleep a little better," I said. "Or maybe once in a while I need to make a movie or some music more interesting. That's all."

"Well, you wouldn't call the cops if you were holding, were you?"

"In Maryland? It's a ticket, basically. Nothing to worry about."

"Yeah, well," he shrugged. "We aren't always in Maryland." He waved at the screen. "Can we get back to this, please?"

"Fine."

I went back to fast forwarding through the nonsense. People came in to the hotel. People left the hotel. Pizza delivery guys came to the front desk and then proceeded on into the hotel, then left.

I wasn't sure what I was looking for—someone acting squirrelly. Someone dropping a single piece of mail off. Someone coming in from another entrance and blocking their face while at the desk. Someone who didn't seem to have a clear purpose.

Whatever it was I was looking for, I didn't see it.

I plunged my spoon into the almond butter and stirred it around. I took the last sip of a long since warmed-up can of cold brew coffee and desperately wished it was beer.

In the chair behind me, Grant had nodded off, the detritus of his convenience store dinner littering the floor around him. I sighed and shoveled it all into the bag, which woke him up.

"You find the bad guy yet?"

"Nope. Doesn't look like there's any pay dirt here."

"Then why'd we waste all this time?"

He stood up, stretching. I held out the bag of trash. When he didn't take it, I stuffed it into the front pocket of his hooded sweatshirt.

"If I knew exactly where to go and what to do in order to *find* the bad guy, this would all be a lot easier. But so far as I can tell, whoever wrote this letter probably didn't drop it off at the front desk. How else does mail get to the company?"

"Could've dropped it off at the show. Maybe slipped it to someone else to bring in a giant package?"

"Fanmail can be dropped off at the show?"

"Sure. People take it to the security guys or the crew all the time."

"Goddamnit," I said. "Why didn't you and Daphne tell me that right away?"

"Uh. You seemed pretty focused on this? And it was in the hotel pile."

"Yeah, but there's nothing saying a member of the crew didn't dump it into the hotel pile when they got back. Who sorts all this stuff? Who is alone with the pile? Who has access to it that nobody oversees?" I stuck my hands over my eyes for a minute, biting back the urge to scream.

"Alright," I said, when I finally dropped my hands, and took a deep breath. "Tomorrow I've got to spend the day talking to as much of the crew as I can."

"Man, they're not gonna like talking to a detective. Even a private one."

"I don't have the time to care about that anymore," I said. "This isn't a one-person job, but I'm the only one on it. So I'm gonna do it."

"Good luck."

We retreated to our hotel room. Grant immediately threw himself on the bed and went to sleep, on top of the covers, with socks on, like some kind of unbelievable freak.

Meanwhile, I debated a "you up" text to Gen, but it was Monday, and she wouldn't be. And even if she was, I was hardly in a position to follow up.

So I settled for trying to write her an email. I got a few words into it before I gave up, deleted the draft, and tried to sleep.

I debated for a long time about what to do with the weapons I was carrying while I slept. The Taser I slipped into the nightstand drawer. The baton I set atop it, right next to my phone, where I could grab it in a moment's notice.

The gun, I locked in the room's safe. I saved the code in a note on my phone labeled "grocery list." The odds I'd need it in the middle of the night were slim to none, and the odds were pretty good I'd just wind up shooting Grant or myself if I went for it in the dark.

Then I sat and stared at the wall and tried to think about how good the money for this was.

It wasn't as comforting a thought as it ought to have been. I was nearly asleep when a bike backfired in the parking lot, or on the street.

Suddenly I saw those Blood Eagle crime scene photos again, and every time I closed my eyes, they came back.

I got the gun back out of the safe and left it in the drawer of the nightstand, right next to the Gideon Bible.

Chapter 30

The next morning we were up and ready for the bus early. Naturally, the bus didn't actually start moving until much later. I had the letter in an envelope, and whenever a member of the crew was standing around, catching a smoke, or otherwise not immediately engaged in crew business, I sidled up.

Nobody recognized the envelope. Nobody remembered taking any fan mail at the show the night before. Nobody even seemed to remember whether they handled the fan mail back at the hotel. Nobody was even real sure how it was distributed.

I grew frustrated with the way I was getting shut out, and I decided to take a more proactive approach. When the bus pulled off the highway into a large rest stop complex, I had dialed in "liquor stores" to Google Maps before we'd even stopped.

My initial plan was to simply grab a bottle of whiskey, but I'd forgotten about Virginia's laws and the existence of ABC stores. The nearest one was three miles away and across some rough country.

I wasn't the kind of runner who was going to make that and be back for the bus. Instead I settled for grabbing a case of Miller Lite and four packs of Marlboro Reds from the convenience store.

Having never been one to indulge the nicotine habit, I was shocked at the amount of cash I handed over. Then I thought about how much

I'd pay to Eddie the weed-farmer/savant the next time I had a couple of days clear and wanted to get pleasantly deranged and figured it was about right, all things considered.

As I started to climb back on the bus, Daphne glared at me.

"We don't like drinking on the bus," she said.

"Good thing I'm not planning to drink any of this on the bus, then." I'd bought it warm anyway, and while I didn't have anything against the odd Miller Lite when I wanted a cold beer, the emphasis needed to be on *cold*.

I tucked it under my seat and settled in for the ride. On previous days I had tried interviewing other wrestlers on the bus, and absolutely none of them would speak to me. Daphne, I think, had instructed them to give me the cold shoulder. I am persistent, but I'm not Sisyphus. I would push on that particular boulder if I had to, but I wasn't going to try and force it just yet.

There was no show that night, so once we'd eaten—Grant at Wendy's, me from the jar of almond butter I'd opened yesterday—I got him settled in the room with the same rules as the night before, and proceeded to get the cans of beer cold, fast. I filled the sink up with ice from the machine, stuck the beer in a can at a time, and spun it.

"What are you doing," Grant said, looming in the bathroom entrance.

"Physics," I said. "Liquid in motion will change temperature more quickly than liquid at rest."

"Huh."

Armed with approximately six cold beers and eighty cigarettes, I went in search of information among the crew. I looked for Braddox first and foremost. If that guy didn't know every detail of how the mail got distributed—of how every piece of equipment and paper and gear that went to or from the venue or in or out of one of his vehicles was dealt with and disbursed—I'd eat my hat.

The way the wind tugged at my head, getting cold, reminded me that I should probably get a hat.

I found Braddox lingering by the truck in the parking lot with a few of his crew.

"Well, if it ain't Mr. Biker, the gigantic pain in my ass," he said.

I only grinned in response. Then I held out a beer. He took it in one hand and opened the ring with just his thumb, which was, frankly, one of the most impressive things I'd ever seen a man do.

"Hoping to talk to you about how the fan mail gets sorted and collected."

He took a slurp from the top of the can and stared at me.

"Look, they tell me the crew collects mail at the shows."

"Do they?"

I sighed. I set down the bag with the beer, and pulled one of the packs of cigarettes out of my pocket and offered it to him with the top open.

He took one and stuck it in the corner of his mouth. "I'm more of a Camel man," he said. He pulled a lighter from his pocket and lit up. I put the pack away and let him smoke and drink for a minute.

Then I brought out the envelope and held it up where he could see it through the plastic bag.

"This was waiting at the hotel yesterday. Surveillance there isn't bringing me anything. Any idea if it was collected at the show?"

He held out a hand, smoke streaming from the corner of his mouth. I let him take the bag and he held it up close to his eyes, squinting.

"Dunno," he said. He held the envelope back out.

"Is this entire company determined to be as unhelpful to my investigation as possible?"

"Look, kid," Braddox said. "I've got one job to do. Get everything off the truck, then get everything back on the truck. That's it. Is anything missing from the truck? Then I'll care."

"So how does the mail collection work?"

"Same way the fucking ballots work I guess, for the MVP bonus cash and shit. They just stuff it into one of those boxes anytime during the show. They're at all the exits. We give all that to the security people and they sort it."

"Why does security sort it?"

He shrugged. "Anthrax? Mailbombs?"

I sighed. "I sincerely doubt that DWF employs anyone with the chemical or biological warfare expertise necessary to detect anthrax in a letter. Explosives, maybe," I added, with a shrug. Braddox laughed.

"Look, kid," he started again, and I fixed him with about one-third of a hard look. He laughed that off. "Alright. Not kid. Is it Jack, or Dixon, or what?"

"Let's go with Jack."

"Jack, you've been given a job to do. I get it. But the company ain't gonna make it easy for you. All they want is that kid to get through the tour alive. You manage that, they'll pay you, you go home. Chances are ain't no one gonna try and make good on these threats. Why not just go along for the ride?"

I struggled to come up with an answer for that. Clearly that was the easy route. Just lay back, be reactive to any unlikely threat, and collect a nice big check at the end of it all.

"Just not how I work," was what I settled on, though I thought it failed to fully convey the personal philosophy behind it. The philosophy that had me living on a houseboat, with no assets, no degree, and only a tenuous connection to something called a career. That wasn't much. But it was all I had.

"I get it," Braddox said. He stuck the cigarette in the corner of his mouth and finished off the beer around it. Then he slapped me on the shoulder with his empty hand. "You ever looking for more honest work, you come talk to me. Can always use somebody got legs and shoulders like yours."

"Thanks," I said. I wasn't sure exactly where "roadie for a wrestling show" rated in my fallback plans if private detective stopped working for me. Probably below line cook in a chain restaurant. But above re-enlisting.

It was time to go see Daphne.

Chapter 31

I waited till the bus was underway before ambushing Daphne.

"Fan mail collection at the venues has to stop."

"Excuse me?"

"That's not all. Anyone turning over fan mail at a hotel should have to leave a return address or it shouldn't be accepted. That's maybe asking a lot of hotel staff but it's pretty basic stuff."

"Where the hell do you get off making demands like this? You're not going to tell me how to run my show."

"Bring it back after I figure out whatever's going on with these threats. But surely you have to see what a gigantic hole in security that is."

"Our fans like the ability to vote on the MVP each show."

"Let 'em do it online, then. But unless you're able—and willing—to hire a bunch of extra security whose only job is to stand and watch the mailboxes and be alert about it, ready to ID anyone who drops in a threat? You've got to shut it down."

"Not sure you should be making ultimatums as it is," she said.

"I was promised cooperation. None of the talent will talk to me. You won't meet me halfway."

"Major disruptions of business are not cooperation."

"Not collecting fan mail for a few nights is hardly a major disruption."

"What makes you think it's only going to be a few nights?"

"The threats all have to do with Virginia, right? So I expect to be particularly on my toes the next few nights. Maybe not so much in Fairfax, but down in Front Royal, Richmond…that's the likely spot for anything to happen."

"So if nothing goes down by then, I can put the boxes back out?"

"I wouldn't. But I'm less worried about angry great-grandsons of the Confederacy in Pennsylvania than I am in Virginia."

Daphne took a deep breath and looked out her window for a moment. "Fine. We'll put a halt on it. I'll see what I can do with the hotels. But make no mistake," she said, turning back to me. "The talent is going to know who is responsible for taking this away."

"That's fine," I said. "Not really concerned with what people think of me."

"I can tell."

With that I decided a retreat was in order, and went back to my seat with Grant, and back to reading my fantasy epic.

Chapter 32

I read while Grant slept. The fantasy epic was not gripping me, but it was better than the highway or the wrestlers that wouldn't talk to me.

Grant was suddenly yanked out of sleep by the bright, brassy fanfare of his phone ringing from an incoming call. It took me a moment to recognize that the ringtone was the fight song of our alma mater.

I guess only his alma mater, technically, as I hadn't graduated.

He stared at the screen stupidly before answering it and immediately cracking a giant yawn into the ear of whoever was talking. I could hear the voice, slightly tinny in the phone's speaker, loud and concerned.

"Everything's fine, mom, I'm fine. Don't pay attention to whatever the blogs say."

My head snapped up. My stomach started churning. I waited for Grant to finish assuring his mother that everything was indeed fine, and hang up, before I cleared my throat.

He looked at me expectantly.

"Grant," I said, "you want to check out a wrestling blog called Squaring the Circle?"

"Oh, I love that one," he said. "He actually covers us. All about the local scene, you know?"

"Yeah. Why don't you pull it up."

He did just that, and almost immediately his face brightened, and not just from the glow of the screen, but from the huge smile that broke out on his face.

"Well, hot damn," he said, "I'm on the front fucking page of Squaring the Circle! I'm the top goddamn story!"

Grant immediately paraded into the aisle, brandishing his phone at everyone on the bus—breaking up card games and ending naps, showing his phone to a host of bewildered and annoyed fellow wrestlers and employees.

With a sigh, I looked it up on my own tablet.

"DELMARVA DEATH THREATS: U.S. Grant Traveling with Body Guard" read the headline and the kicker beneath it.

"God. Dammit."

I opened the article and scanned it, my rising anger not allowing me to absorb any too much of it.

What I could read, I didn't like.

"…angry fans are not new to the world of professional wrestling, but threats of death and harm are few and far between. Surely this is the first time a regional promotion such as the DWF has been forced to hire round-the-clock personal security for their talent.

"DWF have hired professional bodyguard and investigator Jack Dixon, of Elkton, Maryland, to investigate these threats. Dixon has been spotted at the two most recent DWF shows by our own field reporters; in at least one case, sources have referred to Dixon having a special operations background…"

I had to close the folding case over the tablet and stop reading. I leaned back in my chair and closed my eyes for a moment.

Grant came bouncing back into his seat, a huge grin still plastered over his face, brimming with excitement.

"Man, I can't believe it. The heat I'm gonna get for this…"

"Heat? You're fucking excited about this?"

"Of course I am."

"Grant," I said through clenched teeth, "now whoever is making threats knows you have security. They know who I am. Thank Christ, at least there isn't a fucking picture of me. But this puts us at a serious goddamn disadvantage."

"Look, man, you'll handle it. But this is gonna make for some *electric* crowds."

Grant did not seem to see the threat at play here, and I wasn't entirely sure what to make of that. I'd never had a particularly high estimate of his intelligence and it was dropping by the second.

"Your confidence in me is flattering, if completely and totally unwarranted," I said through still-clenched teeth. "But anybody who reads this article is going to know I'm there. They're going to recognize me. And if they mean you harm, they can try and get me out of the way first."

Daphne, having quietly watched all the hubbub from her seat at the front of the bus, came stalking back toward us.

"We can make this a win-win," she said with a smile. "You get to stay close to Grant. And we get to make use of the publicity."

I didn't have the faintest idea what she meant, but I could tell I wouldn't like it if I figured it out.

Chapter 33

"**N**ope. No way. Not happening."

We were backstage in a Kent County theater and I could hear the crowd outside chanting "DEL-MAR-VA. DEL-MAR-VA."

Daphne smiled. "You're a part of the show whether you want to be or not, Dixon. If you go out there in with the crowd, they're already between you and Grant and anybody with a smart phone knows who you are."

As much as I hated to admit it, she was making sense.

Which is why I was stuffed into a dark gray suit a crew member had purchased at a thrift store. I was wearing the Kevlar under the jacket but over the cheap white dress shirt that went with it. I had the gun under my arm, the Taser visible on my belt, and the baton up my sleeve.

I didn't like any of this. I was in over my head already, and we weren't even in the area the threats were located in.

But I didn't see any options. "Fine. But I need to be in the clubhouse with Grant."

Her grin went full Cheshire Cat. "Good. How do you want to be billed?"

"Billed?"

"You know, announced."

"I don't."

She leaned back, looked me up down. "Mystery bodyguard. I can sell that." She tugged at my lapels. "They could've gotten you a suit that fits, at least."

"Haven't met the off-the-rack suit that does," I said.

"Well, I did some work in costuming. Tailored my own tux. I can do some work with it later. For now?" She checked a watch tucked subtly under the cuff of her dinner jacket. "Showtime. Welcome to the world of managing."

She marched out into the cheering.

I marched a few steps down the corridor and thumped a knuckle on the door with the sign that said 'Clubhouse' on it.

It opened a crack and a face appeared: Blake's.

"Talent only, man," he said, the first time I'd heard something approaching antagonism in his voice. He started to close the door but I wedged a foot inside it.

"Not anymore. If I'm managing, or whatever the fuck, I need to stay next to Grant's side all the time. I'm not going out in the crowd and then running towards him. That'd be ridiculous and cause a panic."

Blake tried to stare me down. He was at a disadvantage, namely that I knew just how much of a toll his passion had taken on him. I didn't really doubt that I could shove him out of the way.

"Go on, let him in." That was Grant's voice, slightly muffled. Blake swept the door out of the way.

I wasn't entirely sure what they'd been protecting. Nobody actually dressed in the place; nobody was preserving their modesty. It was the largest backstage room. Against one wall a small buffet was set up; mostly fruit, sports drinks, various kinds of water making health claims it couldn't back up, and some bowls of nuts.

In the middle of the room there were folding tables with some card games going. On the wall was a monitor with a closed circuit of what was going on in the ring, with the sound on high enough that anyone who wanted to pay attention to it could, though it played out of a couple of tinny speakers set high on the wall.

A card game was in progress on one of the card tables, with Derrick Rigg, Spitfire, Caliban, and Grant playing something that looked like Whist. I wasn't too interested in the rules.

Caliban glared at me over his hand, the cards looking like matchbooks in his gigantic hands, but Grant grabbed his attention. I gathered from the flurry of activity at the table that they were partners in this particular game. There was money on the table. Not huge money, but certainly more than anybody's per diem.

There was a knock at the door; someone quickly silenced the TV with a remote, and all other conversation stalled. Cards were held in midair.

A black polo-shirted crewmember with a headset and a clipboard stuck his head in the room.

"Grant, you're not leading off tonight. Caliban and the Twin Terrors, you're up."

The enormous man set his cards down and stood, still glaring at me.

I smiled at him. He was probably pushing seven feet, sure. He likely had eighty to a hundred pounds on me. And no matter what his body fat percentage might be, once he had all of that moving in any given direction, it'd be awfully hard to do anything to discourage him.

But it wouldn't do to let the rest of the talent see me sweat.

And if he really was interested in making a ruckus, I was the one carrying weapons.

He brushed past me on his way to the door, followed by his tag-team competition, a pair of guys who were definitely not brothers, but wore matching masks anyway.

That seemed to suspend whatever game was going on. Cards were set down, money was left in place, and everyone walked away from the table.

I could read a little of the dynamic in the room. Grant had some kind of swagger, which seemed unusual. Blake had appointed himself the doorman, leaning against it with his eyes trained on the TV.

But Derrick Rig was the center of power in the room; he was holding the remote.

You couldn't slip an important fact like that past me.

He also had a cell phone he kept looking at. I would've liked to know what had captured his attention but I didn't want to appear too nosy. I thought about walking over to the buffet—I'd have to pass by him—but that presented problems.

First was that it would stretch the etiquette of my being in here in the first place.

Second was that I really didn't want anything on that buffet table.

Third was that Derrick was at least a couple inches taller than me, and peering over his shoulder was going to be an impossibility.

Besides, it seemed remarkably unlikely that he had anything to do with whatever was happening with Grant. He was the star of the show; he was relaxed, calm, in command of himself and everything around him. And if that blogger who'd clocked me had it right, he was soon to be leaving for greener pastures anyway.

I saw no motive for him being involved in any threats against Grant. I'm not sure I saw motive for anyone in the company to be making threats. I certainly couldn't eliminate any of them.

Hell, the only people I *could* eliminate were me and my boss. A suspect pool of every single person in the states of Maryland, Delaware, Virginia, and Pennsylvania will run a lonesome detective ragged.

I decided not to worry too much about Derrick and focus on reading the room. Blake was doing his sentinel-of-all-that-is-right thing. Spitfire and Night Witch—I didn't know their real names, as they tended to keep to themselves—were looking at their phones in a corner, occasionally leaning close and sharing a laugh at something on one of the screens.

There was no singular mood in the room. Everyone was getting ready to work, and that was a different headspace for everyone.

But no one—not even Grant—was worried.

Here we were with death threats against a member of their company, and clearly nobody cared.

I wandered over to Blake. He looked at me, eyebrow raised, clearly curious.

"Anybody here worried about any of these threats?"

He shrugged. "You're gonna be a professional, you learn to put shit aside."

"Well, sure. Everybody has bad days and still has to go to work, but…" I trailed off, looked around to see if anyone was listening in or paying attention. Everyone was in their own world.

"Well, most people's job isn't as dangerous as ours," Blake said. Then, with a chuckle, he gestured at the vest I was obviously wearing underneath my ill-fitting suit. "Present company excluded, I guess. But if you are not totally focused on what you're doing in the ring, you can get hurt. Worse, you can hurt the person you're working with." As he said this, unconsciously, his eyes flitted toward Grant.

I nodded and went back to watching the monitor, the action of which was too small for me to follow.

Some time passed. I sweated in my suit and my vest, and finally, someone knocked on the door and called for Grant and Blake.

Out in the corridor that led to the stage area and the ring, the cheering of the crowd became a dull roar.

Grant put on his hat, adjusted the hang of the vest he wore, and was handed a Confederate flag from a stage hand. Grant held it out to the guy, who delicately snipped the top and bottom of it with scissors he pulled from a toolbelt. Grant looked at me and shrugged.

"Makes sure I can rip it in half in one go, right?"

Then we heard Daphne, from the ring, boom out the words "U.S. GRANT."

He turned to me and winked. "Two steps behind me, bro," he said, and set off.

I counted his footsteps and followed, trying to keep focused and not completely and utterly lose my shit.

Just before I went out a stage hand grabbed me and stuck a Bluetooth headset in my ear. "What the hell?" I glared at him.

He shrugged. "Daphne's orders. Says it completes the look even if it's not connected to anything. These, too." He handed me a pair of dark plastic sunglasses.

Those, I could possibly use. I certainly wasn't going to see much of the crowd past the stage lights without them. I put them on and hurried down the tunnel just in time to see Grant vault himself over the top rope with flair, climb the post, hold up the Confederate flag, and rip it in half.

The crowd erupted, a mixed chorus of booing and cheering.

It was going to be a long night.

Chapter 34

The heat of the kevlar and the suit in the dressing room was nothing compared to the heat of it out in the arena, under the lights. It wasn't even that big of a house, but it was packed straight to the rafters. Between the heat of the crowd, the lights, and the pressure of being in front of that many eyes, I thought I was going to drop from dehydration before we'd been out there for three minutes.

Grant went through his whole routine with the flag, talking about the Union, downplaying and trash-talking the Confederacy.

"Rebels shouldn't get memorials," he was shouting. "Losers don't get statues in my book!" The crowd was lustily booing as he threw the torn flag to the mat and ground into it with the heel of his boot.

"The only place this flag and everything it represents belongs," he was saying, really getting into it, biting at the words, throwing the crowd's energy back into its face, "is in the trash!" With that cue, a stage hand held out a metal trash can to me, and I dutifully passed it over.

Inside there were already a few scraps of flash paper, to make sure that the flag burned, or at least that it *looked* like it burned.

As I watched the crowd I realized that Grant was *good* at this, or better than he'd been the first time I saw him do it. Everyone likes an energized audience.

I tried to pay more attention to them than to him, which was tough. He was pretty magnetic, and I don't think anyone was more surprised by that than me. I saw a lot of folks yelling, some people waving signs I couldn't read, but I didn't see anyone coming out of their seat, nobody holding a weapon, nothing that rubbed me any wrong way.

I was so busy studying the crowd I didn't realize Grant was talking about me until his hand landed on my shoulder. He was handing me the trash can with the smoldering remnants of the torn flag in it.

"Some people don't like hearing these truths," he shouted. "Some *cowards* assume I'll be just like them, and shut up the first time someone threatens me. Am I scared? Have I stopped?" The crowd roared, "No!"

I took the trash can and handed it down to a waiting stage hand, who dumped a cup of water in it and spirited it away down the tunnel.

"But the company…the company needs to protect us, you know? They've go to watch over their investments. So they went and got me the finest bodyguard money could buy." He slapped me on the shoulder. The crowd cheered.

"Any of you cowards out there want to try anything, think twice," he yelled. "My boy Jack is ready for you!"

I hated this. I hated it beyond words. I never liked thinking about crowds at wrestling meets, and those were pretty tame compared to this one. I did my best "stoic movie extra portraying a bodyguard," keeping my face completely neutral, hands at my sides, idly scanning the crowd.

The attention shifted off of me pretty quickly once Blake came out to a smattering of applause that sounded almost polite compared to the response Grant had gotten.

Then the real show started.

Grant was into it, this night. Their early clinches and exchanges of blows had a sharpness to them that I hadn't seen before. Early on Grant had Blake in some kind of come along hold via his shoulder and dragged him to the corner, dramatically waving at the crowd, getting them to their feet, before slinging Blake across the ring into a complicated series of off-the-ropes moves.

I stayed put in the corner, watching the crowd, but occasionally I was drawn into the match. At one point I heard an honest to god slap—not the ghost blow complete with stomp on the ring to make a sound, but the real contact of flesh on flesh.

I turned to see the imprint of Blake's hand across Grant's cheek, white and livid. Both of them looked furious; Grant with being struck and Blake about whatever had caused him to lash out.

They came together in a clinch and I strained to hear anything they said to one another.

I didn't catch anything, but when they came out of it, Grant was focused on their wrestling and not on the crowd. It was only a matter of moments till he lifted Blake up and slammed him down again, then pinned him.

Grant stomped around the ring, urging the crowd on, whipping them into a frenzy, until he took his black cavalry hat and tossed it into the crowd.

Blake had already made his exit by the time Grant stamped down the tunnel. I hurried after him, wondering if I was going to have to get between them. Given the state Grant was in, I didn't like my odds a whole lot.

Once in the safety of the tunnel, Grant came right for Blake, who was leaning against the wall.

"What the fuck was that?" he growled, getting right in the older wrestler's face.

"Playing to the crowd is great," Blake said, "until you're paying more attention to them than to the wrestling. That's how people get hurt."

"Then fuckin' say something instead of slapping me. You made me look like a bitch in front of the entire house."

By now, stage hands were wandering over, wondering if they were going to have to break it up.

"You wouldn't have listened just to words," Blake said, finally and forcefully backing Grant away from him with his hands on the inside of the younger man's shoulders. "But you did listen to the slap."

"But the crowd…"

"Fucking loves you," Blake said, pointing back down the tunnel. "You put yourself over, really, for maybe the first goddamn time, kid. Pay attention."

Then Blake walked away, presumably to the trainer's room, for his usual ice and whirlpool treatments.

I followed Grant to his dressing room, convinced that Blake was right.

Chapter 35

The next ten days passed exactly like the previous week. A bus ride, a night in a bad to mediocre hotel, crappy road food, hotel gyms, and Grant constantly updating me on the buzz he was getting on the blogs and message boards.

The matches all went the same way, too. Grant was really getting into it now, feeding off the energy of the crowds.

I hated every second of getting out there with the crowd. I stared out from behind the thick sunglasses they'd given me, tried to peer through the lights to look for anything threatening.

When we got to Centreville, Virginia, I was low on supplies and bribed the roadies into unloading It for me. I went out on Route 29 until I found a Target that I just hoped would stock some of the Wild Friends nut butters I was currently living off of. I had found that I couldn't talk myself into a chain restaurant or fast food burger more than once a week, and even then I felt sick about it.

Luckily, they did, and I sped back to the hotel with my backpack full of almond and peanut butter, a small sack of apples, and a case of beer for the roadies. I hated where I was and what I was doing. I hated that I hadn't had the deck of the *Belle* under my feet for two weeks. I hated that I hadn't seen Gen in that time.

But the one part of all of it I could control, like usual, was what I ate. So at the very least I was going to do that and try and keep myself sane.

Being back in the saddle helped. I should, by now, have taken back and apologized for every harsh word or thought I ever entertained about bikers. Well, the riding part, anyway. The one-percenter lifestyle was still a big lie, your basic criminal enterprise dressed up in costumes and fancy words about brotherhood and freedom.

But actually being on the bike, on the road, even in the early onset of winter? Nothing compared to how it felt to be that in control of my destiny. Part of me wanted to get back on Interstate 66, head down to 81, and see how much of the country I could see.

But that part was a hell of a lot smaller and less vocal than the part that wanted to finish this job, get paid, go home, and figure out what to make Gen for Christmas.

By the time I'd pulled back up to the hotel, given the road crew their case of Miller Lite, and gotten back to the room, Grant was napping.

But Daphne was waiting for me outside the hotel room with an envelope in her hand.

I held my shopping in one hand and my helmet in the other, so I looked at her rather than reaching for it.

"Really? Another one?"

She nodded and jerked her head to the room's door. "Let's go wake up Sleeping Beefcake."

I unlocked the door, giving him a courtesy knock—three loud raps against the door—as I opened it. When I flipped the lights on he was only just waking up, stretched out on top of the covers in his jeans and sweatshirt.

"Do you two have the goddamn AC on in here?" Daphne shivered. It was true that the room was right around meat-hanging temperature. I was used to this kind of cold, having spent the past two winters on the *Belle* without a whole lot of working heat.

"Sorry," I said, "habit." Grant had turned over and pulled a pillow over his eyes, groaning at us to go away.

"Mail call," I said. I went to the side of the bed and ripped the pillow off his head, chucking it against the wall. "Get up or get ready to eat a cold, wet washcloth," I said. Daphne brought the letter over. I took it to the bathroom, got out my pocket knife, and carefully cut it open at the seal, tipping it over the sink.

All that slid out was another piece of printer paper. I grabbed a fresh Ziploc bag from my luggage and carefully picked it up, reading as I walked back out to Daphne and Grant.

"This is basically identical to the last one," I muttered. "Some added stuff at the end about being patient, you haven't listened, when you least expect it, blah blah." I waved it in the air and Daphne reached for it, but I pulled it away.

"Prints," I said. "There's still the chance this becomes a police matter and we don't want you getting popped for it, do we?" Using another Ziploc over my other hand I got the letter inside the bag and smoothed out so it could be passed around. I looked at it again. Something about it nagged me. Nothing much had changed except that paragraph at the end, which I reread.

You have ignored our warnings. And our previous letters on this tour. Be prepared for retribution when you least expect it. We are patient.

"Odd," I said, as I turned the Ziploc over to Daphne. "It's almost identical. Just got that added paragraph. And it mentions letters *this* tour. But this is only the second one."

"Yeah well, you can't expect idiots like this can count, right," Daphne said. Grant laughed. Clearly they were ready to dismiss a discrepancy.

I wasn't.

I didn't know what it meant, but it didn't make sense. Furthermore, it seemed like the threat had been revealed to be nothing but a bluff. Here we were in rural Virginia, where the threats were said to emanate from, doing the exact thing the threats said not to do.

And all that had happened was another letter, practically a cut and paste, with an added paragraph that didn't quite fit.

"You know, Grant," I said, "it sure seems to me like we've called their bluff. Tomorrow's what, the fourth show in Virginia? And not a damn thing has happened."

"You're not quittin' on me, are ya, Jack?" Grant, still sleepy-eyed, looked genuinely worried for a minute.

"He isn't," Daphne answered for me. "Is he?" A sharp look in my direction.

"Of course not. I'm on the job till the problem is rooted out or the tour's over," I said. What I meant was that I was on the job as long as I was still logging billable hours.

"Great," Grant said. "Besides, we're fucking killing it lately. Wouldn't want to lose you as part of my corner."

"I'm not part of your corner, Grant. I'm not part of the show." The problem was, I had basically let myself become part of the show. And I didn't see a way out of it. I held out my hand and took the letter back from Daphne, storing it carefully in a larger bag with the other one we'd gotten. I still didn't like any part of this.

Grant yawned and stretched. "Is it dinner time?"

Daphne laughed and wandered outside, crooking a finger at me to follow, which I did.

I pulled the security latch out so the door wouldn't lock, but we'd get some privacy. She looked up at me sharply.

"You're thinking something."

"I'm thinking a lot of things."

"Gonna tell me what any of them are?"

"I don't work for you," I said. "And I'm not sure what it is I think yet."

"The hell does that mean?"

I shrugged. "Investigative work does involve hunches. But usually a 'hunch' is based on seeing a missing piece of information."

"That doesn't make any damn sense."

I thought over how I'd said it and realized it didn't. "I mean…I see a hole where information should go. I realize that there is something I need to know and don't, and can determine a vague outline of it…but not enough to make any intuitive leaps."

"You're no Sherlock Holmes, then, I take it."

I snorted. "Sherlock had all of his cases meticulously plotted for him by a benevolent deity," I said. "All of his clues carefully placed where he and only he could see them. I'm looking for stuff anyone can see, but not everyone would notice. I also lack a sidekick. World of difference."

She laughed. "Fine. Don't share it with me. But the company's paying a lot of money for you, and hasn't seen any results yet. It may not be my company, but on the road, it's my responsibility."

"I got it. And the instant I have anything actionable, I'll loop you in. But I don't." Only a niggling suspicion that something isn't right. "Now if you'll excuse me, I've got a phone call to make."

"Oh? To your boss?"

"My girlfriend."

"Same difference," Daphne said, taking the last word as she wandered away. I didn't contest it.

Chapter 36

I went carefully back into the hotel room, where Grant had fallen asleep again. I dialed Gen's number, snuck into the bathroom, closed the door, and sat on the only available seat.

"Who's this?"

"Very funny," I murmured carefully. "I wish I could call more, but..."

"I know, evil doesn't rest, neither can you."

"Well, trust me, when this job is over I plan to do nothing but rest for at least a week."

"Jack, that's a bold-faced lie and we both know it."

"Well, okay, but the gym and visiting you both count as rest."

"Only if you're doing it all wrong."

"Jesus, I miss you, lady."

"I miss you, too. How's the job going?"

I looked in the direction of Grant's gentle snoring. "So far, so good, I guess. I'm still standing ringside with him, which I hate."

"Are they making you wear wrestling gear? Maybe just boots and trunks? Because if they are, I want pictures."

"I'm afraid it's just a suit and a Kevlar vest."

"I can do without the vest," Gen said. She was certainly aware that my job could turn violent, and wasn't thrilled about it.

Neither was I.

"It's just for the look of the thing," I said. "I doubt I'm really going to need it at any point."

"Good. You are to come home unperforated."

"Yes, ma'am."

"Now I like the sound of that a lot more than Kevlar. You can keep that."

"I will remember that." I paused. "Ma'am."

She laughed. I liked the sound of it; it was rich and inviting and I missed her so much right now I was ready to drive four hours on cold roads back to Wilmington to see her.

But I had a job, and I had to do it.

And at that precise moment, my job had woken up, called my name, and said, "It's dinner time, man, come on."

Gen heard. "Is that Grant?"

"Yep."

"He sounds fun."

"It is a nonstop delight. I've gotta go, Gen." I paused. "I miss you. A lot."

I cringed. Was that really the best I could do?

"Miss you, too. Go do your job," she said.

That seemed like a win. We hung up. I walked back out into the room, took my jacket, checked my gun and my taser, and went with Grant to find the nearest acceptable dinner place.

Chapter 37

It occurred to me while we walked that I'd gotten far too accustomed to carrying a firearm. The pepper spray and the Taser didn't bother me as much; those were extremely unlikely to kill someone. The baton, well, that felt like something I could rely on *and* that relied on me. It wasn't going to kill someone by accident, or at a moment's whim.

But the gun under my left arm was too snug, too easy, too comfortable. I couldn't lock it up or leave it behind, but I made a note that after I got home, I was going to ask Jason for a couple of cases that didn't require one.

But that was later and now was now and the gun was a fact of my life. Until I could figure out what was nagging me.

We wound up at a chain restaurant that specialized in burgers, and I ordered one with a fried egg on it. Grant did the same, though he also ordered a beer and was well into his second basket of endless fries. I stuck with water and nothing.

Fries were the very devil, as far as I was concerned. Grant noticed me staring at the basket and pushed it towards me.

"You know, it's supposed to be a bottomless basket for everyone at the table."

I held up a hand, palm out. "I'm good."

"You'd think you were trying to make weight for a meet."

"I am, it's just called outliving my father."

Grant laughed. "At least you could have a beer. I know you drink a little."

"I do, but not when I'm working, like right now."

"You can't eat just a couple of fries?"

"That's not how it works with me, Grant." I had guided the hostess into giving us a corner booth where I could see the door. It opened and I focused on it. Just a gaggle of teenagers. They were unlikely to be a threat.

"Whaddya mean that's not how it works?"

"I mean I can't just eat a couple of fries and go on with my day. Especially not when unlimited fries are on offer."

He snorted and stuffed a last handful into his mouth. When he was *almost* done chewing he said, "Just takes some willpower and discipline, man."

I got very angry, very quickly. It must've shown in my features as I leaned across the table, because Grant's eyes widened.

"Don't talk to me about discipline. I live like a fucking *monk* compared to you. And I don't go looking for extra help in the gym when my own work won't cut it." I was hissing through my teeth by the end and Grant looked stunned.

Suddenly there was a presence leaning over the booth. Some bodyguard I was. I snapped out of my seat and put myself between Grant and the grinning, slightly pimply teenager who'd been getting out his phone.

I had stopped *just* short of grabbing his wrist and turning it back. Thank God. The last thing I needed was to assault a minor in a Red Robin.

"Hey, is that U.S. Grant?" the kid asked me.

"Yeah, it's me," Grant said. "You want a selfie?"

"Yeah, I do," the kid said. "Is that okay?"

"Yeah," I said. "It's fine." Grant slid out of the booth and the kid came out of his own. He held out the phone to me and I looked at him like an idiot for a few moments before I finally realized he wanted me to take the picture for them. I took a couple shots, one upright, one landscape, and handed it back.

"Keep giving rebel flag waving idiots what for," the kid said. He and Grant fist bumped. It was a heartwarming moment. The kid then looked at me and said. "You're the bodyguard?"

"Something like that."

"I bet you were like, special forces or something, right?"

"I was a cook."

The kid looked at me dubiously. Then he suddenly broke into a grin. "Nah, you're just saying that as, like, cover, right? Because you can't say what you really did."

"I fed sailors and Marines for four years. I never did a single glamorous or noteworthy or dangerous thing, except operating kitchen equipment while hungover."

"Yeah, I get it, gotta live that lie." He held out his hand for me to fist bump.

"Don't take this as me acknowledging that anything you said is even remotely correct," I said when I reciprocated.

Grant was beaming as we walked back to the hotel. It was getting colder and I wanted to stay out in the night air, like I would've if I was at home on the deck of my boat.

"What was that shit about not relying on my own work ethic in the gym?" Grant said.

"Eh, nothing. I'm just in a bad mood. Sorry."

"You know, just because you do a cycle once in a while doesn't mean it gets easy. You still got to put the work in."

We were just outside the hotel and my frustration was close to boiling over.

"Grant. The last thing I want is a goddamn primer on effective steroid use. You do it your way, I'll do it mine. Let's just go to bed. There's a show tomorrow night."

"I'm all jazzed up, man. A kid asked for a selfie! I've got fans. We've gotta go somewhere. Maybe there's a club."

"Nope. No. No. No." If Grant dragged me out to a club I would end up using that gun on me or on him. Maybe both.

"Come on…"

"Does the company have a curfew rule?"

He got quiet.

"I will narc on you *instantly.*" I pulled out my phone.

Sheepishly, he went into the hotel.

Chapter 38

The next night's show was one of the biggest, noisiest, most miserable moments of one long miserable experience.

What was worse was that there was going to be an autograph lineup after the show, in the lobby of the theater. I was going to have to stay "on" and focused on the crowd for an extra hour for people who'd bought an extra package with their ticket.

Grant once more got huge noise from the crowd. He got better every time they got louder, and this arena—at a small college outside of Richmond—was absolutely rocking.

It was a great show for them; even Blake looked happy about it. I found myself standing behind Grant as he signed autographs, let fans take selfies, and generally hobnobbed with the crowd.

He was good at this, too, at ease and calm and just basking in the adoration.

I was idly scanning the crowd, looking at faces, looking for groups, looking for anything out of place.

Then I saw it. A fleece jacket hung up on a tactical holster hanging on the side of someone's belt, with a boxy-looking European style handgun in it.

He was in Grant's line, and he was holding a stack of paper in his hand.

I didn't hesitate.

"GUN," I yelled, as I launched myself over the table, bulled past the people in line, and grabbed the guy. I didn't want to tackle him, send the piece scattering. Who knew if it was on safe or what might happen if he dropped it. But I did get his gun-side arm and twist it up behind his back, walk him over to the nearest wall and strip the gun out of his holster before he could respond.

People screamed and scattered. The papers the man had been holding had fallen out.

The guy I'd pinned against the wall was half my size—in decent shape, but a skinny runner's body. He had not been expecting me to vault over the table at him, and he was in no way prepared for what happened when someone my size and with my grappling training got that close that fast.

And he was blubbering. Adrenaline was pounding in my ears, so I didn't really hear much of it, but a few words did sink in.

"…open carry state, man…"

* * *

Luckily, the fan, name of Neil, thought it was kind of awesome that he'd been rousted by his new favorite wrestler's bodyguard, and agreed not to cause any trouble for me or the company in exchange for free signed photos of all the talent, t-shirts, and tickets to two future shows. All in all the company got off cheap.

I simultaneously felt like an idiot and sort of competent. I had spotted a guy with a gun and subdued him immediately.

This was not, however, something anybody in the company was prepared to let go of any time soon. When I walked past any of them they threw themselves up against the wall, assuming the position, or put their hands up to dramatically signify that they weren't carrying.

Grant was able to relax and laugh through it all, flying on how well the show had gone for him.

"Man, you're lucky that guy just wanted some tickets and swag," he said, sliding onto his bed and picking up the remote.

"Everyone's lucky I didn't really hurt him. I'm not sure how I didn't."

"You were just doing your job, man."

"Yeah, well, in open carry states the company needs to start a weapons policy or something," I said. I sat down on my bed and placed my hands on my knees, firmly, trying to keep them from shaking. A deep well of black exhaustion was opening up underneath me.

"Dude, your arms are shaking."

"Yeah."

"You alright?"

"Yeah," I repeated. "I'm fine. Just an adrenaline spike, you know? I was ready to really throw down with that guy once I saw the gun. And then all this adrenaline's got nowhere to go."

"Yeah," Grant said, nodding as if he understood. "You, uh, is there anything I can." He paused. "You wanna talk about it or…"

Christ, no. That was the absolute last thing I wanted to do. "I don't much like hurting people," I said. "Though the job means sometimes I do. I'm not used to it."

"You used to hurt people plenty back in the gym, man," Grant said. "Shit, people *hated* practicing with you."

"There's a reason I quit wrestling, Grant," I said. The shaking in my arms had subsided and the tiredness was rising up to claim me. I shook my head to clear my vision. "A lot of reasons. You're gonna stay put if I fall asleep, right?"

"Yeah. Shit, I don't wanna get my arm dislocated when you throw me up against the wall."

I looked up sharply. Grant had turned pale and held his hands up. "Sorry, man. Sorry. Just making a joke."

I didn't say anything. I kicked off my boots, set the gun in its holster on the nightstand, took off my shirt and jeans, and just went straight to sleep.

Chapter 39

The next day on the bus was all the same kind of jokes, at least for the first hour. It was a long ride, all the way up into Pennsylvania for some shows in and around Reading. Not exactly the Aesir's home turf, but a hell of a lot closer than I liked. I had emailed Bob and asked if he could give me information on their known clubhouses and the like, hadn't gotten anything back yet.

As I got on the bus, everyone put their hands up on top of the seats in front of them and stared at me, giggling.

I ignored them, took my seat next to Grant, and tried to get lost in reading. It worked, for a while. Every now and then someone would make some small gibe about checking a passing car for guns, that kind of nonsense.

I was able to tune it out until Daphne came by and nudged my seat with the toe of her boot. I elbowed Grant awake, since she had a business face on.

"Local TV station in PA wants to do a package on you," she said, pointing at Grant. "Including stuff about the threats, your bodyguard, and so on. Probably worth doing."

"Oh, hell yeah it is," Grant said, at almost the same time I said, "Absolutely not."

"This is going to be a company decision, not a security decision," Daphne said.

"Well, I'm not going on camera. That's not in the terms of any agreement you signed with my employer," I said. I was desperately hoping that was actually true, as I had no idea.

Daphne tapped her finger against her chin. "That's how we can spin it, then. You can't appear on camera for security reasons. We'll give 'em some of our tape from the shows and cast you as a mystery man."

"That's not really going to have the operational security effect I was looking for."

Daphne shrugged. "Too bad. We own that footage, and you've been appearing in front of our cameras for the last week and a half. Stuff's been uploaded to our YouTube channel, our website. We might even start streaming shows if we can get a sponsor for 'em."

"I'm still not talking to local news," I said. "I won't be on camera for them. It's a goddamn security risk for multiple reasons."

"What," Daphne said, smiling, "you got enemies, Jack?"

"I might." My thoughts about wannabe Viking bikers had receded, but every so often I found myself staring hard at a group of bikers through the bus window, looking for the symbols on their cuts.

"Man of mystery spin it is, then," Daphne said, "for anyone watching local news. But anybody who knows how to use the internet will see your face just fine."

"I'll take what I can get," I said.

* * *

The news crew was waiting at the hotel when we got there, having set up in one of the dingy conference rooms available. I stood around in it while Grant got makeup applied. The producer asked me if I needed any and I had strongly indicated that I would not be appearing on camera so no, it wasn't necessary.

"Not even in the background, looming a little?"

"No," I said.

"It would make for a great…"

I didn't like being rude, but I turned my back to her and walked away. My patience and capacity for being around this many people for this protracted a time period was drawing perilously thin. I was going to get in a real fight with someone, with real consequences, if I didn't find a way to get my head screwed back on right.

I needed a proper gym, a proper cocktail, a proper bunk, and a date with Geneva Lawton. Not necessarily in that order.

I projected enough anger while Grant was doing his interview that nobody else from the local broadcast team tried to talk to me again. After it was over, Grant shocked me by expressing a desire to work out, so we were off to the hotel fitness center. He engaged in what looked like an exhausting routine with the heaviest dumbbells the room had, then bouts of pushups, and isometric exercises.

He worked up a good sweat, I'd give him that. I sat in a corner and sulked. I hated that I was doing it. I hated being here. I hated myself and this job and everything about it.

"You gonna sit in the corner and sulk, or are you gonna get some work in?"

The fact that even Grant noticed shocked me a little bit out of my stupor.

"I'm not sulking."

"Yeah, you are," Grant said, breathing a little hard while doing push-ups. Then he curled his left hand behind his back and kept doing them. "What's the matter? Angry that I'm getting all the press?"

"I couldn't care less about that."

"All could've been yours. Shit, man. You could've gone to the Olympics. Could've been somebody. If you'd cared." He paused for breath, and switched to one-handed push-ups with his left arm. "As much about wrestling as you did." He fell to his knees, striving for breath. "About…whatever it is you're doing right now."

"You know what, Grant? If you want me to care about what you have to say, my rates are going up."

He popped back to his feet, sweating and breathing hard. "You think you're better than me, huh? Well at least I fuckin' finished what I started. I graduated."

"Yeah, with a degree in what? Some bullshit so fake they won't even let you be a P.E. teacher in a middle school in Iowa, of all godsforsaken places."

"Christ, you're an asshole," Grant said, and he strode determinedly out of the gym. I followed him quickly, not letting him outpace me despite the difference in our natural strides. He tried to slam the hotel room door in my face, but I caught it with my boot and kicked it back open.

"Sure, I'm an asshole," I said as he turned to face me. "But I'm still getting paid to babysit you. So that's what I'm goddamn well doing."

Grant just shook his head. "Don't even need this anymore," he muttered, as he walked towards his bed. I wasn't sure what that meant, but the drive for confrontation seemed to have gone out of him, so I left it there. I got out my tablet and alternated between mindless surfing and trying to read a book.

His phone buzzed; he flipped on the TV and navigated to a local broadcast, where his segment on the news came up. He didn't say anything, but he sat up, beaming. An anchor came onscreen, chattering about pro wrestling and death threats.

In the video package that accompanied it, I was *clearly* visible at ringside, in my suit and vest, looking around the crowd. If you knew what you were looking for, you could see the gun under my jacket.

Then Grant's face was onscreen, huge and sweating, answering banal questions. Until they asked him point blank if his bodyguard was part of an "angle," and the interviewer made the air quotes with his fingers.

"Absolutely not," Grant said, grinning. "Jack Dixon is an old wrestling teammate of mine, a decorated veteran, and a crack private investigator and security guard…"

"Jesus, Grant," I said, falling back on the pillows of my bed, "what the fuck is that about?"

"Gotta play it up while it's working," was all he said.

I tried to ignore the TV for the rest of the night.

Chapter 40

It was a tense day until show time. Grant was pissed at me, and I was pissed at me, and I was pissed at him. It was a real triumph of camaraderie and good feeling.

We made it till that night without talking to one another. Come showtime, we still weren't talking, but there I was in the room anyway, waiting for him to go on. His match had been pushed back even further, going on just before Rigg and Spitfire. In fact, that morning he'd spent some time working with people other than Blake; it looked like the boy was moving up in the world, or at least the ranks of his regional promotion.

For a moment when I saw Blake watching their training earlier in the day I wondered about bitterness as a motive, but there would've been no reason for him to be bitter back at the start of this tour, when Grant was distracted and lazy in the ring.

Hell, if anything, the guy looked proud. He probably should be.

Later that night, in front of a thumping crowd, I watched Grant turn in the performance of the tour so far. He had them in his hands by the time his intro was over. His match with Blake was crisp, clean, and they both sold every bit of it. They both even went off the ropes at one point, something they'd practiced, but hadn't done before.

Despite myself, and my determination to be angry and hate

everything around me—something I was perversely good at—I was impressed. And I was determined to tell Grant and Blake that when we got back.

Grant went straight to his dressing room, and I started to follow him, when one of the stage hands grabbed me.

"Guy here to see you," he said.

I assumed he meant Grant, and that I should vet him, so I followed him just a few steps away.

When the wheelchair rolled up, I reminded myself to not sound patronizing, and generally not to act like an asshole. That was proving to be difficult for me, lately.

The man in it put his hand out, and I shook it.

"If you wanna see Grant, we can probably do that," I said, "but it might take a minute. And I'll need to...search any bags or anything."

The man in it—he looked about my age, clean shaven, with thick arms and shoulders full of muscle mass and definition, and atrophied legs—chuckled a little.

"Not here to see Grant. Here to see you, Jack."

Then I looked again, closer, and he held up his all-access pass on its lanyard.

"David Rackham," I said, as I read the words. "Holy shit."

"Those aren't exactly the words I would've thought you'd say, but you know..."

"Jesus, David. David Rackham?"

"Last time I checked."

"What are you doing here?"

"I live here. Well, not far, anyway."

"Yeah, but..."

"Well," David said, staring at me from under his Phillies cap, "you might not be shocked that your name is a little memorable to me. That I notice it if I hear it."

"Yeah. I guess...you would."

"Yeah," he agreed, his voice taking on a little edge. "It's hard to forget the guy who broke your back."

I winced. David smiled up at me, but it was, to put it mildly, a sarcastic smile.

"Look, David…can I call you David?"

"Why not."

"I feel like you and I ought to sit down and…" I stopped, and put my hand over my eyes.

He actually laughed, but it wasn't a particularly mirthful sound.

"I owe you. Something. A talk, an apology, a…"

"Yeah," he agreed. "You do."

"I guess that's why Grant sent you the tickets. Smarter than I give him credit for," I muttered.

"Grant?" He dug into a pocket of the fleece jacket that sat over his lap and pulled it out. "No. No Grant. The tickets and passes came from…Troy? With a note to make sure to say hello to you, and how glad he was to see you on TV. They even sent a note addressed to you. I didn't open it," he added, as he held out the small envelope.

My heart and stomach couldn't decide whether to sink to the soles of my shoes or exit through my mouth. My hand was shaking as I reached out to take the card-sized envelope he was holding out to me.

"David, I'm sorry, but I gotta go." I dug in my pocket and tossed a card at him, then turned and bolted down the corridor.

The door to Grant's dressing room was hanging wide open and no one was in it. Two chairs were overturned, and a towel lay in the middle of the floor. I looked for the exit signs, followed them down the maze of corridors. I felt a draft.

A black-shirted staffer was slumped against a wall near the emergency exit, which was open—but no alarm was going off. I didn't see any blood, and he had a regular pulse and shallow breath. Probably had taken a big blow to the head.

I raced outside. In the parking lot, I heard engines revving. I drew my gun as I ran, which did absolutely nothing to calm my nerves or steady my heart. I saw taillights moving under the lamp-posts, and I heard the rumble of bikes as they headed for an exit.

Three of them, around something larger. A van.

Goddamn it. Everything suddenly made sense.

Chapter 41

The first thing I did was call Gen.

"Hey Jack. I was just thinking…"

"Gen. I hate to be rude, but I have to ask you to do something."

She hesitated. "What?"

"I want you to pack a small bag and go to Dani's house."

Her breath caught, but only for a moment. "Why?"

"I'll explain later. Dani will understand. I promise this will all be okay in a little bit."

"Jack, I'm not going anywhere till you tell me something."

"It has to do with the Aesir. I don't think they know who you are, but I don't want to risk that."

"Are they back? In touch with you?"

"Something like that."

"Why Dani's house? Why not my parents?"

"Your dad a combat veteran and a martial arts instructor? Because Dani is."

"Okay," she said. "Be careful, Jack. Come home. Un-perforated, like I said before."

"I will." I hated thinking that I might be lying to her.

The next thing I did was make two more phone calls. Then I got hold of Daphne on the hotel line. Then I sat and waited for my phone to ring, or for an email to come. Daphne waited with me.

It took an hour, but the phone did finally ring. I looked over at Daphne, whose eyes were wide. I took a deep breath to still myself, and tapped the screen to accept it.

"Mr. Dixon."

I knew that voice: Jarl Troy, of the Aesir MC. I didn't respond.

"Surely a man of your insight already knows that we hold your friend, Mr. Aronson."

"What do you want, Troy?"

"Many things, Mr. Dixon, only some of which you are capable of delivering."

"Just name it."

"I would, except you are already proven a liar. So I will need assurances."

"Christ, you like to hear yourself talk."

"Swearing by the pacifist god of weaklings, cowards, and hypocrites does not become you, Mr. Dixon."

I decided to clamp my mouth shut and give him time.

"Surely you have not been so foolish as to alert the authorities. If you were to do that, I'm afraid we would find Mr. Aronson's continued care and feeding too expensive to countenance. And, Mr. Dixon, please understand that we are very well connected in this area. We will *know* if you contact the police. Then I will call you and you will listen as my seax takes a finger off Mr. Aronson for every one of my men you have taken from me."

"No cops. I got it."

"Yes. In time you will be provided with an address. You will go to that address—alone. We will be observing the route in. Once there, you will surrender yourself."

"Go on."

"Do not complicate this matter, Mr. Dixon. You owe us considerably. I did not like using Mr. Rackham in this plot. I will not like moving on to your family and friends. Such things ought to be beneath men."

"No part of that told me how we get Grant back."

"Once we have you, we'll discuss ransom for Mr. Aronson. Are we clear?"

"Crystal."

"Good. Do keep this line open." There was the silence of dead air, and then the screen of my phone lit. I looked at Daphne, who had gone pale.

"That didn't sound good. We gotta call the cops."

I shook my head. "I don't think that's a good idea. From what he just told me, I think they're wired in. I don't know if that means crooked cops, or some kind of tap…but it doesn't seem like a good risk."

"I thought the threats were in the south, in Virginia," Daphne said. "This doesn't make any sense."

"This has nothing to do with those threats." My voice was much, much calmer than I felt. I sat still on the hotel room bed, breathing carefully. I wasn't sure what came next, but some part of me was waiting for it, reserving my energy.

"What do you mean?"

"This is about me. The people who took Grant are coming at me. Not at Grant, not at your company."

"Then why…"

"Because my name and my face were on the goddamned news, and all over the internet." I took out the card David Rackham had given me, which I'd slipped into a plastic bag. I scanned the lines again.

Mr. Dixon,

We have been building quite the picture of your habits and acquaintances. We have no wish to hurt Mr. Rackham. He was an expedient tool to demonstrate our reach and grasp; we know you and your life, and if need be, we can reach out to people you care about more than a wrestling opponent whose back you broke. We know where you live and the places you frequent. We know where your family lives. Your friends.

Do not prove yourself a coward by putting them in danger. Wait for our instructions and even Mr. Aronson will live.

Troy.

"What do I tell Mr. Gogarty…"

"Well, I already told him plenty. He was the second phone call I made."

"What," she stood upright, fear suddenly replaced with anger. "Why the hell would you…"

"Because he's responsible for this bullshit. Him and Grant. The threats were never real. It was all a goddamn piece of theater meant to blow Grant's name and character up. That's all."

"What the fuck are you talking about?"

I sighed and went over to Grant's side of the room, where I'd carefully spread out his luggage and clothing. I pulled two envelopes from the top of folded jeans and underwear.

"Carefully slipped inside a compartment cut in the bottom of his weekend bag. I assume this is where the other two came from. He put the last one in out of sequence; it was supposed to be third, not second. That's why it bothered me so much. It didn't make any sense."

Daphne opened the letter I'd handed her and quickly scanned it, then looked up at me, her mouth slightly open.

"This was in Grant's bag?"

"Yep."

"So it was all an angle. One they didn't bother telling us about."

"They sure didn't. And by hiring me, and then putting my name and my face all over, some old…" Enemies sounded grandiose. "Some acquaintances of mine got stirred up."

"So you're saying the people who knocked out one of my security guys and kidnapped Grant are after *you*."

"Yeah."

"And what're you gonna do?"

"Fix it."

"How?"

I took a deep breath. "This is gonna sound like some dumb bullshit, but it's probably better if you don't know the answer to that question."

"What're you gonna do, Jack, track them down and shoot them all?"

I didn't answer.

She stared at me for a moment before looking away.

"I don't know how many of them there are," I said, and decided that I probably needed to assure her a little. "So, you know…probably not *all*. I'm not about to hand myself over to get cut into dog treats and saddlebags. But it is my responsibility to get Grant back."

If saga accounts of the Blood Eagle were to be taken at face value, the lungs could be pulled free while the victim was still alive. I doubted that, but I didn't much want to find out for sure.

"Then what?"

"Not really looking past that part." The snap of ribs figured large in my imagination.

"What the hell do I tell the company? And the fans at the next stop?"

"That really isn't my problem right now."

Daphne stared at me for a while longer, searching for something to say. I opted not to help her look. I wasn't happy that I'd been used, and other than staying afloat long enough to pay me, I didn't give a good goddamn what happened to Delmarva Wrestling Federation. I think Daphne had gotten the point without my saying that.

So I went back to waiting for the phone to ring. It did, the same number as before. Once again, I picked it up in silence.

Troy gave me an address, and some directions.

"And it would be best, Mr. Dixon, to come resigned. And alone."

"Don't worry, I'd hate to have to dig more than one grave."

Troy laughed. "Oh, Mr. Dixon. We won't be needing six feet to bury any of what's left." A pause, but I could hear him breathing; he wasn't done hearing his own voice yet.

"We will expect you tonight. If the sun rises and you've proven yourself a coward, your friend dies. Then others."

He was done; I could tell. I waited for him to hang up. I carefully wrote down the directions he gave me, made a phone call of my own, passed the directions on, and waited twenty-five minutes.

Then I put on my vest under a thermal shirt, my shoulder-rig, the Taser, my jacket and gloves, took my helmet, and went to track down a roadie.

I found a couple of them smoking just outside the hotel lobby, huddled together against the cold.

"Need my bike out of the truck," I said.

"And I need my ass warm and my dick sucked, but ain't neither of those gonna happen tonight," he responded.

I was not in the mood for impediments to my work. I grabbed the far side of his collar with my right hand, tugging it against his neck and dragging him against the wall of the hotel, away from the front doors and the lights. I jammed my forearm across his throat, restricting his breathing just enough to hear him gurgle.

"I do not have the time for your particular brand of petty bullshit," I said, leaning forward and whispering the words while he worked hard to breathe. "Open the fucking truck, or get the keys from someone who can. Right now."

I stepped away. The roadie gasped for breath and reached into his pocket, pulling out a set of keys. Behind me, his buddy had gotten his gumption up; I could hear his footsteps on the concrete as he readied himself to take a run at me.

I turned around, lifting my helmet and catching the downswing of the pocket-chain he'd been readying to swing at me. It was loud;

probably chipped the paint. I didn't have a lot of time to worry about that, so I just stared at him. I took a step forward; he took one back. I took another one. He took another one. And so on until we were back in the light cast by the lobby doors.

He got the idea and turned away. I followed the first one to the truck.

Chapter 42

It was the coldest ride I'd ever taken. There was no joy in it, no freedom, no exhilaration.

I was driving to some kind of reckoning. I'd brought it on myself, sure. I'd gotten casual and sloppy, started to let other people make decisions for me. I hadn't been sharp enough in figuring out the bullshit Grant and his boss had cooked up.

Most of all I hadn't taken operational security seriously enough. Too much time worrying about things outside this job.

"Can deal with all that later, if there is a later," I said aloud, inside my helmet, which was filling up with humidity from my expelled breath in a way it didn't usually.

I was getting close to the spot where the GPS, and the directions I was given, indicated I should turn off onto an unpaved road in an empty cornfield. It went on for a couple of hundred feet, leading to a ramshackle little house. I took in as much as I could as I got close; a car parked in the driveway, a bike parked next to it. A single light on in the house, that looked small and dim enough to be a lantern or a flashlight. I killed the engine of my bike.

Briefly I wondered if it was about to be the last time I'd ever ride It.

A figure resolved out of the gloom ahead of me, suddenly illuminated by a handle-flashlight clipped to the collar of his leather cut. One hand rested near his belt, on a holstered pistol.

"Dixon. Gimme your phone."

I spread my hands out to either side. "Come get it."

"Don't play any funny bullshit with me," the Aesir growled. Despite the beam of his flashlight, I couldn't see much of his face. That would help.

I didn't say anything.

"Gimme your fuckin' phone."

His hand moved uncertainly on the grip of his pistol. He was close enough that he wouldn't miss if he decided to drop me right there, and I was no kind of gunslinger to try and outdraw him. Not with my jacket zipped up. *Stupid*, I berated myself.

Then two quick, loud pops rang out from the house. The Aesir in front of me turned towards the sound, following instinct.

I seized the moment and leapt at him. The baton snapped into my hand. He fumbled with his gun, having lost his concentration. The baton cracked him across the face. I heard the crunch of bone. He stumbled backwards. I landed on top of him, using the baton to bear him to the ground. There was a crunch; something soft gave away underneath the steel bar in my hand.

He gurgled under me, started thrashing madly, no thought of going for his gun. I realized I had the club in both hands and was pressing it down on his throat. I kept it there until the thrashing stopped. And the gurgling.

Only then did I reach down and pull the gun from the holster at his side. I vacillated between tucking it into my belt and throwing it into the field.

I heard footsteps approaching, so I clicked it off safe and pointed it toward the noise, which was a large, armed man coming straight towards me, his steps slow and measured, quieter than you'd think for someone his size.

"It's me, Jack," Brock Diamante—who'd been the third phone call I'd made, after Gen and Mr. Gogarty—whispered. The arm that had taken a bullet a couple of months ago was now wrapped in a soft cast. The barrel of a pistol rested on the wrist, which he lowered so the barrel pointed at the ground. I did the same.

Brock came forward, prodding at the guy on the ground in front of us with the toe of his combat boot. "He done?"

"Yeah."

"What do we do with him?"

I thought a moment. "Let's get him in the trunk of their car. Along with your man."

"Yeah." Brock looked down at the Aesir. "I didn't hear any shots. What did you…"

I didn't answer. We put our weapons away and bent down to pick up the biker.

Chapter 43

I hadn't carried a dead body before. It didn't seem like an experience that would grow on me, even though I got to do it twice in rapid succession.

Brock was ahead of the game; he'd brought tarps.

We patted the two Aesir down for anything useful before we tossed them in the trunk. Neither had usable ID; both had *Utlangr* on their cuts, with local marks identifying the particular branch, I guessed, and some other runic patches that symbolized who knew what. They both had phones and, luckily, one of them was very, very new. We hadn't shut the trunk yet, so I tugged the right arm of the guy whose throat I'd crushed out of the trunk and stripped his glove off.

I pressed the thumb of the ex-biker to the home button when his phone asked for it to unlock, and unlock it did. Then—still using his hand, which I tried hard not to think about, with Brock holding the phone—I opened the GPS and looked for saved locations.

Then the phone startled us by ringing. I looked at Brock "He'll know my voice. You gotta answer it. Just sound gruff and deferential."

"Huh?"

"Lower your voice and say 'yes, Jarl' or 'yes, sir' every time you're asked a question."

I answered the call and held it to Brock, then leaned forward so I could hear it.

"Did Dixon show?" It was Troy's voice, that was clear even from a distance.

"Yes, sir," Brock growled. He did a passable growl, I had to admit.

"Peaceably? He hasn't tried anything?"

"No, sir."

"Odd. I expected more of him. Bring him to the clubhouse. Make sure he is cuffed."

"Yes, Jarl."

"Do this well, Bode, and promotion is likely." The line went quiet. We waited in absolute stillness until we were sure the call was dead.

"So this asshole's name was Bode," Brock muttered, as he tucked the arm back inside the trunk and shut it.

"Not real interested in learning his name," I muttered. I felt the stirring of butterflies in my stomach, but I was able to quash it without having to look at the bodies. Brock seemed to notice something was wrong.

"You gonna hold it together?"

"Yeah," I said, with more conviction in my voice than my head.

"First one, yeah?"

"Yeah," I said.

He shrugged. "Look, uh…if you're planning to club the rest of them to death, I don't blame you, but…"

"Don't worry," I said, "I realize this is gonna come down to a gunfight. I get it. Let's go." I'd kept Bode's phone awake by opening apps, and finally found what had to be the clubhouse in the navigation app, as it was saved as home, was only a few miles away, and had been the most recent starting point, with the desolate farmhouse as the destination.

"Was anybody else in there?" I asked Brock, gesturing towards the house.

"Nah," he said. "Looks like it's deserted."

"Aesir probably owns it. Alright. I'm gonna take their man's bike, you drive their car. Those'll be the engines they're expecting to hear. Here's what I'm thinking, but speak up if you don't like it…"

Chapter 44

In the end, Brock had basically agreed to my plan. I tailed him all the way to the clubhouse, which, thankfully, was set in a deserted lot far from any town, behind a chain link fence. There was a long, low, single story building and an attached garage, with a quonset hut style roof. A few tall lampposts illuminated the parking lot, but dimly.

Per our plan, we pulled up but stopped short of the garage or the clubhouse, left the engines running, and slipped away from the vehicles. There was a stack of wooden pallets among assorted other junk in the lot, and we met behind it, looking for cover.

"What do we do if they just pop your boy while we're sitting out here," Brock murmured, barely audibly, as we waited, watching the vehicles chugging away in the cold night air.

"I don't think they will. Not about him—it's about me."

Soon enough a couple of guys in cuts came out the side door of the clubhouse. One of them was carrying a shotgun in one hand, the other some kind of pistol with a long clip.

"We're already outgunned," Brock whispered. "Need to decide what we're doing."

"Follow me," I muttered. I crunched my way across the gravel into the open garage. There were three bikes parked, as well as a van. I looked at Brock and held up four fingers, shrugged. He nodded.

We heard some shouting from the parking lot and then boots crunching on gravel towards us. I crouched behind a table full of tools against one wall, held my gun out over the top of it. Brock put himself against the hood of the van, aiming around the side.

The two guys who'd come out to investigate the car came around the corner, illuminated by the lamp post.

I aimed at the one with the pistol. He lined up with my sights, a clearly outlined shadow. I couldn't have asked for a better target picture. I was perfectly stable on the concrete slab of the garage. It was like firing at a silhouette target on the range.

I pulled the trigger, twice, quickly.

The report of the 9mm inside the contained space of the garage was incredibly loud. He went down, crumpling around the bullets in him, groaning, his gun clattering onto the gravel outside.

Brock shot as well, the report now deafening, but the biker with the shotgun had ducked around the corner for cover and put himself out of Brock's sight picture. He stuck the pistol-grip around the edge and fired in blindly.

The sound of the pistols was nothing compared to the sound of that scattergun. I heard the shot pinging against bikes, the van, tools. I felt small bites tear into the side of my arm, my boot. I moved up along the tool-rack I was leaning against, squeezing off careful shots into that corner, one, a second, a third. If nothing else, I was keeping his head down.

Brock moved up from the van and shot straight through the side of building, three quick blasts. I heard a miserable kind of grunt and then a sound of something heavy clattering on the ground.

We came around the corner. The guy was down, but weakly raising the shotgun. I kicked it out of his hands, then bent to pick it up.

Grant did the same with the long-clipped pistol the biker I'd shot had dropped.

I bent down to the guy with the shotgun. His eyes were rolling, blood welling up around his hands.

"How many of you are here?" I asked.

He tried to make some kind of defiant gesture. I shrugged and stood up, slinging the shotgun over my back and moving to the door that led into the main clubhouse. Brock tapped me on the shoulder. I turned around and he pointed at himself, then around the corner of the building. I nodded, and he trotted off at a smart pace to the front entrance.

I felt nagging pain in my foot and my arm, but I kicked the door open and bulled in anyway.

Inside it looked like a cross between a renfaire merchant and a standard MC clubhouse: a pool table, crossed axes and swords on the wall, various Viking-style round shields painted in different colors, all with the raven skull that was the club's main symbol. There were large, brown beer bottles scattered around the table.

There was a biker with a gun crouched behind the pool table, but he wasn't looking. He would've had adequate cover if I'd been low, but I wasn't. I opened up on him, squeezing out rounds as I was coming through the door.

The top of his head exploded. I came forward, around the pool table, up against a ratty leather couch, kneeling behind it. My foot was now barking at me in a serious way. My shoulder ached from holding the gun up, even with my elbow resting against my jacket. I heard other shots from the front of the building. They sounded to me like the report of Brock's pistol, but I wasn't any kind of expert.

"I PRESUME THAT IS YOU, DIXON?"

Troy came marching out into view, from one of the rooms in the back. He had one long arm wrapped around Grant, who was dirty and disheveled, a bruise closing one eye, a gag in his mouth and zip tie cuffs around his wrists.

Troy's other hand held some kind of knockoff AK with a folding stock, currently tied up against the barrel of the rifle, the muzzle pressed into Grant's ribs.

"One more step, I'll open him up," Troy said. His only eye was wild and wide, his voice—normally a powerful, controlled instrument—clearly coming unhinged. It was hoarse. "Put your gun down or he dies."

"That doesn't help you," I said. "And while you're busy doing that, I get a clear shot. There's only one way you come out of this alive, Troy," I said. "Step away from him, put the gun down." I realized I was yelling, my hearing dimmed by the gunfire.

"I am not quite that foolish," Troy said. It sounded like he was talking from behind a glass window, or through a poor microphone from some distance.

"This is between you and me, Troy. Put the gun down. Step away. You and me. One to one."

"No. No. I will not be lured into that."

Brock came into view behind Troy, not ten feet away, gun leveled.

"If he moves at all, kill him," I said. Troy seemed to tense up, his finger curling inside the trigger guard of his AK. I was ready to try for an unlikely shot. Brock was like a damn statue behind him, gun resting on the soft cast. The muzzle didn't move a micron. Mine, on the other hand, was swaying everywhere. My foot was numb; the inside of my riding boot was slick and wet.

Troy's eye widened. Then he seemed to realize the game was up. He uncurled his hand from the gun he held and his arm from around Grant, who immediately ran away, wisely seeking cover behind some furniture.

Theatrically, Troy lowered his rifle to the ground and stepped away from it, holding his hands out. He was still smiling. I kept my gun trained on him.

"Fine," he said. "Call the authorities. Take me into custody. Men will come forward to take the fall. I'll be free in days," he said with a sneer. "And I will be coming right back after you, Jack Dixon. I'll start with the man you crippled. Then your family. Your friends. Because this world lacks will, and vigor, men like me can take whatever we wish…"

He was cut off by the sudden report of a pistol.

Mine.

I shot him carefully and deliberately through his eyepatch. He crumpled to the ground, all his limbs gone limp. Six and a half feet of crazed biker cultist hitting the bare concrete floor of the clubhouse all at once was louder, somehow, than the shotgun had been. I moved up and looked down at him.

He'd been dead before he hit the floor, but he looked surprised nonetheless.

Brock holstered his weapon as he came up to me, standing over the body of Jarl Troy. I did the same with mine. Grant let out a string of expletives from behind the couch.

"What the fuck now?" Brock said.

I bent down and picked up the AK with my gloved hands. "Time to make this look right. Better, anyway."

"Yeah," Brock said. "I gotcha. They emptied this at us from ambush."

"Yeah," I said. "Gimme a second, though," I said, holding up a finger, before hobbling as fast as I could out to the parking lot to puke.

Chapter 45

"We had approached the meeting to negotiate in good faith. We heard a warning from inside, and then the AK opened up just a tad bit too early," I said, for the third time, to the local detective who was currently interviewing me. "Otherwise my associate and I would both be dead."

"And you called Mr. Diamante, rather than local authorities, because…"

"Because I was working under the mandate of the company that had hired me," I said.

"And the two of you…despite being taken by ambush…engaged in self defense measures that resulted in the deaths of five members of the Aesir MC?"

"I wasn't counting," I said. "Just trying to stay alive."

At that moment the door of the interview room opened and a woman wearing the kind of fancy athleisure sweatshirt that probably cost as much as my riding jacket came in. She was tanned, fit, hair in a neat bun, and immediately in charge of any room. In my slight daze I didn't quite recognize her.

"Melanie Hanes," she said, positioning herself between me and the detective. "Mr. Dixon will not be answering any further questions, as he is wounded and in need of medical attention."

I'd been bandaged, and a paramedic had pronounced me unlikely to die of lead poisoning any time soon, but I wouldn't have minded a trip to a hospital, and a hospital bed. I was ready to collapse.

Ms. Hanes turned and slipped me a card and muttered, "Don't say another word."

"Now, come on, counselor, we…" The detective was cut short.

"Mr. Dixon has been engaged in strenuous, dangerous activity against criminal elements *your office* has failed to contain despite the clear threat they posed to the community. If Mr. Dixon is not being held or arrested, we are leaving right now. Think carefully on your next words, detective."

He said nothing. Ms. Hanes motioned me to my feet, which were leaden. I followed her out of the room and then out of the police station without either of us saying another word.

In fact, she didn't even look at me till we were in her car, a sleek dark gray Lexus.

She started up and was out of the parking lot before she spoke.

"Let me see if I can address your questions." I hadn't asked any, but that didn't slow her down. "I was contacted by your employers, Mr. Clark and Ms. Dent. I am not working for free, but at a significant discount given the regard my daughter holds for you. Your motorcycle was collected by employees of the DWF and will be transported back to Maryland, or released to you, your choice. Now, to ask you some: do you need to go to the hospital?"

"Almost certainly."

"I thought as much." She asked Siri to navigate us to the nearest hospital. "You're not going to die in my car, are you?"

"Nah. Not even bleeding anymore. But I'd like these wounds a little more professionally dressed. Where's Brock?"

"Mr. Diamante has already been released and I believe is planning to secure nearby lodgings until you're ready to return home."

"You also representing him?"

"Yes. Though it seems extremely unlikely that either one of you will be charged with anything. The Aesir MC are, or perhaps were, a notoriously violent and dangerous criminal conspiracy. This cannot have been a secret to local or state law enforcement. Most will likely be secretly thrilled that their senior leadership is gone. You did them a favor."

"Everybody's hero," I muttered.

We drove in silence after that. The check-in process at the hospital was long and tedious, as usual. My insurance situation was fluid, at best. Ms. Hanes seemed to think she could pressure the DWF into covering it, since I was working on their behalf.

The hospital decided to hold me overnight; once I was in a room, Ms. Hanes joined me.

She pointedly held up her phone, and turned it off. I did the same with mine, setting it on the bedside table.

"Mr. Dixon; did the firefight at the Aesir clubhouse go down as you described it to the police?"

I bit my lip as I considered the question. She read my hesitation almost immediately.

"Are they likely to discover serious discrepancies between your account and the available physical evidence?"

"Let's put it this way; the account they have and the physical evidence will match up well enough that they can run with it as is if nobody decides to look *real* close."

"Good. I assume you and your partner are professional in…these matters." She cleared her throat.

"Troy…their Jarl, club president, whatever…intimated that he had contacts in local law enforcement."

"He almost certainly did, but those contacts are unlikely to come forward and burn their careers in order to defend his memory. If anything, they'll lie low in the hopes that nothing about them comes out."

That seemed like a fair assessment to me. And exhaustion was creeping up. Despite my best efforts, I cracked an enormous yawn.

Ms. Hale stood up. "Sleep is the best healer, Mr. Dixon. I'll check back with you in the morning. I expect you'll be able to return home in a day or so."

She left, and I fell into a dark sleep that I wished was dreamless.

It was filled with echoing gunshots, the roar of a shotgun, the top of a head exploding behind a pool table. A huge one-eyed man collapsing on a floor.

I woke up in a cold sweat, shaking, not sure of where I was. Slowly, it returned to me. My shoulder ached; my foot hurt. I shuffled in the bed and the lights from the street moved as a car passed by.

And only then did I realize that someone else was in the hospital room with me.

Chapter 46

I reached for the call button, but it and my phone clattered to the floor as the figure was suddenly on top of me. I caught the glint of metal as light from the window showed me the seax he dramatically raised.

I was tired, and I was weak, but I wasn't going down without a fight. I caught a glimpse of a blue shirt, and then the knife was plunging down towards my chest. I caught his wrist with my left hand and pushed it away. He'd been aiming to punch through my sternum, into my heart. A killing blow. I didn't have the strength to stop it, only to push several life-saving inches to the side. He still sunk the first couple inches into my shoulder—the one that had taken buckshot.

He wasted the other hand shoving it over my mouth and leaned down close.

"Jarl Troy isn't dying alone," he hissed. I heard the crackle of a radio on his shoulder: a cop, or maybe a paramedic.

I got him by the throat with my right hand. I started squeezing. As hard as I could, given the state I was in, that I'd been given medication, maybe that wasn't hard enough. He had leverage. That knife sank deeper into my shoulder, and it hurt more than anything else ever had.

He kept leaning on it. I swear I could feel my heartbeat pinging against the blade.

But I still had my hand on his throat, and I was still squeezing. Fear rose up in me. And there might have been some adrenaline left in me after all, because my grip got stronger, and tighter.

I heard a crunch; I felt something crumple under my fingers.

The pressure on the knife eased, but he left it in my shoulder. He started thrashing, trying to get away from my grip on his throat. His flailing arms managed to rock the knife back and forth. I heard it ripping me open as he knocked against it. My right hand was locked around his throat, my fist cramping, my arm screaming like I was at the end of three hours in the gym. My left hand was clamped around his wrist, and apparently kept him from doing anything more interesting with the knife than wobbling it back and forth a little.

It hurt beyond description.

But I wasn't letting go. Maybe Jarl Troy wouldn't die alone, but I didn't plan to either. The thrashing got weaker and weaker, until finally he clattered to the ground.

I felt weak, and faint. I looked over at the knife that was now hilt-deep in my shoulder. I reached for it, intending to pull it out.

I blacked out as soon as I touched it. The last thing I heard was the hard, terrifying scree of one of the machines attached to me.

Chapter 47

More blackness. More dreams of gunshots, of shotguns emptying in a crowded garage, of heads exploding on pool tables, of sharp-edged knives.

Occasionally music intruded on them, some of my favorite Van Zandt songs. Some that I knew Gen liked, by First Aid Kit and Grace Potter. Others I wasn't sure I could identify.

When I blinked awake, slowly, the bright lights of the room hurt my eyes.

I was slow to lift my head up; there were two other people in the room with me. One large and hulking, sitting on a couch against the wall. Brock.

The other, smaller, slimmer, blonder, all around more fun to look at, stepped to the bedside and grabbed my hand.

It took me a moment, in a drugged haze, to recognize Geneva Lawton. But there she was.

"Hey," I said slowly, my mouth dry and sore.

"That the best you got?" She smiled, but it was a frightened smile. I squeezed her hand.

"This wasn't what I had in mind for our next date," I said.

"It'll do," she said. "For now."

Brock lumbered into view. He looked down at me. "You're

apparently a hard goddamn man to kill, Jack," he muttered.

I wanted to reach up and smack him; Gen was right there. But my left arm wouldn't move the way I wanted it to. I looked over and saw it was thoroughly bandaged and immobilized.

"Yeah, had to have some surgery there. Docs say you'll be fine, but that knife did a number on…"

"Shut up, Brock," I muttered.

He looked at Gen, and then had the good sense to look sheepish and flush a little. "Why don't, I, uh, step out…"

He left the room and I held on to Gen's hand for a while.

"How long have I been out?"

"Couple of days," she said. "Brock called your boss, your boss got hold of me. I took a week. Is there anyone else you want me to call?"

"Dani, maybe."

Gen let out a nervous chuckle. "Jack, I drove up here with her. You sent me to her place, remember? Should I call your parents, maybe?"

I thought about that one for a moment, then shook my head. "Nope. No way to escape my dad as long as I'm bedridden. I'll let them know in good time."

She twisted her lips in what I recognized as uncertainty, but I knew, beyond a shadow of a doubt, I didn't need to be around my dad right now.

"Okay," she said, and we lapsed into silence a moment. "You want to tell me what happened?"

"Not unless you want to hear about me killing three or four bikers," I said quietly. I wasn't sure if it was three, or four, or maybe five now. I didn't much want to know. After I said the words I started to shake. I closed my eyes tightly. Gen bent down over my bed. I wrapped an arm around her.

"I really don't," she muttered. "But if you need…"

"Nope," I said. "Just this."

* * *

A few days later I found myself in Jason's office, back home in Maryland. At his conference table, in a three-piece dark suit with a thin chalk stripe, sat Mr. Oscar J. Gogarty, owner and CEO of Delmarva Wrestling Federation.

He was a little greasy looking, a little creepy, and far too pleased with himself, if the smile plastered across his too-bronzed-for-December face was any indication. His silvered hair was swept back from his temples, his white French-cuffed shirt was spotless, and he looked for all the world like a captain of industry rather than the owner of a regional wrestling promotion.

"I'm afraid that bill is not negotiable any further, Mr. Gogarty," Jason was saying. He was dressed to go toe-to-toe with the man who was trying to stiff us. I was in jeans and a thermal shirt, my arm in a sling.

I looked like hell and I knew it. I was mildly hungover, and I hadn't slept more than an hour without waking up sweating, or shaking, or both. I had bags under my eyes, a week's worth of stubble along my neck under my not-groomed-in-too-long beard, and an orange Orioles cap jammed on my head, even though we were indoors.

"The thing is, your man did not fulfill the terms of his contract with us. Our employee was kidnapped. And he did not complete the tour. Revenue fell quite short of projections." He was so smug. So pleased with himself, sitting at the end of the table. If the BMW he'd come in was any indication, he could easily afford what he owed me.

But men like him didn't get rich by writing checks.

I was not, to put it mildly, ready to swallow any of his bullshit. So I led with my strongest card.

"You walk out of here without writing me a check, the first thing I'm doing is calling the writer for Squaring the Circle and spilling everything I know. About why you didn't want cops involved, about how the entire goddamn notion of threats was made up by *you* and *Grant Aronson* to generate heat for his character. And I'll tell him about every illegal thing I saw on the tour."

"You can't prove that…"

Jason pulled out a manila envelope and removed the letters I'd taken from Grant's luggage after the kidnapping. "We can certainly muddy the waters enough that you come out looking bad," he said, laying the envelopes and letters down on the table.

"This is blackmail. Extortion," Gogarty sputtered. "I won't stand for it."

"No," Jason said. "This is an employee who almost got killed because of your disregard for the notion of consequences."

"Blackmail would be if we held this evidence over you," I said. "And demanded regular payments. Which, as tempting as it sounds, seems like it would be exhausting. Pay me what you owe, and I go away. You never hear from me again."

"Those letters don't really prove anything…."

I got out my phone and started ostentatiously dialing. I set the phone on speaker.

"Hello?"

"Hey, Tommy Wilkerson, Squaring the Circle?"

"Yeah?"

"This is Jack Dixon. We met at some DWF events…"

Gogarty's eyes got wider.

"U.S. Grant's bodyguard? You know how many questions I want to ask…"

"Prepared to give you some exclusives depending on…"

Gogarty rushed down to the end of the table, grabbing for my phone. He managed to shut it off.

I caught his tie with my good hand and pulled him down till we were eye to eye, our noses touching.

He didn't like what he saw, and I didn't blame him. His nose wrinkled. I didn't blame him for that, either; if I could smell my own breath I'm sure I'd have hated it too.

"You split the fee into three checks, make them out to cash. You fucking got me?"

I spat the words through gritted teeth.

He nodded, vigorously. I let him go and he stumbled away, instinctively smoothing out his tie and his vest. I felt a little bad for ruining the line of his suit.

"When those checks clear," I said, "you get the letters back. I go away. Is that clear?"

"Yes," Gogarty said. Now, slightly humbled, he tried to regain his composure as he opened his briefcase and removed a corporate style checkbook and a silver-cased fountain pen from inside his suit.

* * *

"Who're the other two checks for?"

"Brock," I said, "and David Rackham."

"Who's David Rackham?"

I was staring at the checks Gogarty had written, moving them around, rearranging them with my hands. They were large. Not as large as one single check with all three amounts folded into it would've been, but I was keen on giving Brock his due for the assist. And I guess I thought a nice check could buy out some of what I owed David Rackham.

"The last guy I ever wrestled against in college," I said. "I broke his neck. Or his back...some important part of his spinal apparatus. He hasn't walked since. Ran into him in PA. Aesir used him to distract me."

I thought a moment, and said, "But you knew who David Rackham was, because you would've researched all of that before you hired me."

"Sure did," Jason said. "But I think it was important for you to say that out loud."

"Maybe. I should look him up again."

"We should all do a lot of things."

"Yeah."

We were silent a few moments. Jason gathered up the papers on his table and scooted them back into the manila envelope.

"Learn some things about yourself, first time you're in a real firefight. First time you shoot at someone who's shooting back."

I was silent.

He went over to his sideboard, to the French press. Poured two cups from it, both of them steaming.

"World ain't going to miss those men, Jack," he said. "The sooner you realize that, the better."

"I learned I was right not to like guns. Makes it too easy. Too cheap."

"Mmm," Jason said. He brought the mugs over to the table and set one down in front of me. I looked at it. Then I looked up at him.

"If I hadn't had it, I might've done this differently. Maybe fewer people would be dead."

"Maybe you'd be the only one."

"Maybe. I think I did learn something, though."

Jason sipped his coffee. "What's that?"

"That I don't think I can do it again."

"Normal to think that," he said. "Won't know until a next time."

I stood up, leaving the coffee untouched, taking two of the three checks.

"Won't be a next time," I said. "I quit."

The End

Jack Dixon will return in **DOCTOR'S NOTE**

About the author

Daniel M. Ford is the author of *The Paladin Trilogy*. A native of Baltimore, he has an M.A. in Irish Literature from Boston College and an M.F.A. in Creative Writing from George Mason University. He teaches English at a college prep high school in rural Maryland.

Find him on Twitter @soundingline.